THE FIRST TRUE THING

THE FIRST TRUE THING

CLAIRE NEEDELL

HARPER TEEN
An Imprint of HarperCollinsPublishers

And if the earthly no longer knows your name,
whisper to the silent earth: I'm flowing.
To the flashing water say: I am.

—Rainer Maria Rilke,
from *The Sonnets to Orpheus*,
translated by Stephen Mitchell

THE FIRST TRUE THING

ONE

COVER FOR ME. *Told Mom I'm w/you. Senna too.* I stare at the text from Hannah and toss my phone on the bed. The last thing I need is to let myself get pulled into Hannah's shit.

I know a promise to cover for Hannah is a promise to lie. I've already sworn to Mom and Dad and everyone at the Center: *No more lies.* It's the sort of thing they'd make me leave Group for. Lying for someone who's dealing, using, or putting themselves in harm's way is definitely a "violation." They'd make me leave, go back through intake, and reapply to the whole program.

They'd say I'm not ready. Kevin, my addiction specialist, told me at intake that the hardest part about Group would be showing up. At first I thought he meant that literally. Now I know that being a member of the Peer Support Group for New Living means being like one of those foul-smelling frogs we dissected in freshman-year biology. Every afternoon in Group, it's like I'm being sliced open and stuck with pins. It turns out that *showing up* at the Center means letting everyone see the weakest, worst parts of you. They say they want to know my story. They say it's a *safe space*. But I've noticed it's often in the most frightening places that people insist you feel safe.

It's been two weeks since I started at the Center, and I admit that I still want to drink. I still think that drinking made me happy. Or, at least drinking made happiness seem possible. It's like the feeling you get when you're little and someone hands you one of those paper birthday party invitations, or a sparkly Valentine's Day card. A beer is like that for me. It's something bright and shiny that is already *there*. A drink is right in your hand until another takes its place, each with the same exact promise. I haven't forgotten the feeling, not yet. They say I will.

I've tried to explain in Group about the night of my Death Wish crash. Maybe it was just the full moon, but I remember as I rode away from Andy, there was a kind of brightness in the woods, a light I was chasing. It's like the light I always felt inside me with the first shot of vodka. I could see the same brightness, the same light in Hannah's face when she did lines—not at the end of a coked-up binge, but in the beginning, when the night first began, and everyone was up. It was all electric then; it was all light. Everyone chased it all summer long, and the more we chased it, the darker everything actually got.

Now, I'm living in that place between the darkness and the light. Everything has slowed down. Andy and I have started talking more at school again. But since I'm grounded and sober, nothing can really happen. I can't chase anything—not the light that my first drink of the night always promised, and not the darkness that followed.

I take a deep breath and stare at my reflection in the mirror above my dresser. My hair has gotten long and loose, it reaches down to the middle of my back in coppery curls. Back in middle school, I hated my hair, and got up early every morning to straighten it, but now I think it's my best feature—that and being tall. But I can't say I'm at my best tonight. I have dark circles under my eyes, and my skin, which is usually clear, is blotchy and broken out. But the real problem with my appearance is the scar across my chin. I had the stitches out last week, and I've used the ointment Dr. Hagan gave me to keep the wound from drying out and creating a deeper scar. Mom got the best plastic surgeon in the county. Dad talked like I didn't deserve it.

"She nearly breaks her neck she's so drunk, and you're worried about the size of the scar on her face, Jude? That's not right." They were in the hospital room a few feet from my bed, talking in loud whispers.

"She'll already be living with this the rest of her life," Mom said. "She'll be living with this alcohol issue the *rest of her life*."

"At least she'll have a rest of her life," Dad said.

I was quiet and shut my eyes, so they didn't think I was listening. When they left the room to talk to Dr. Hagan, I wiped the tears from my cheeks. Then the three of them came back into the room, and Dr. Hagan sat at the end of my bed, like I was a little kid and he was going to read me a story. He said I didn't need to go away to rehab. "You can get treatment right here in Waverly," he said in his steady doctor voice. He left the white-and-green brochure for the Center for New Living by my side.

I thumbed through the glossy pages. There were pictures of counselors with ugly glasses and weird L.L.Bean–looking clothes, and there were pictures of teenagers drinking soda and eating chips, sitting around long tables talking, looking serious and sad. I didn't know what scared me more—not drinking, or having to talk to the people in the pictures.

I finger my scar. It doesn't hurt anymore, but the skin feels rougher than the rest of my face. At the Center, they tell me I'm an alcoholic and that I'll always be one. But I'm sixteen, and that's too young to be anything forever.

I stare out my bedroom window at the ink-dark sky, the silver, nearly full moon. The tops of the trees seem to glow in the beam of the streetlight, their branches waving in the strong, warm wind. It rained hard all morning, but brightened in the afternoon. I lean over, open the window wide, and take a deep breath. It's so warm it feels more like spring than fall, except the air smells of musty old leaves—dead things, not things coming alive.

They say at the Center that you don't keep your secrets, your secrets keep you. I think I know what this means. I almost died the night of my Death Wish crash. When I felt myself begin to fall, and I no longer felt the bike beneath me, I felt free. I'd been

4

trying for months not to fall, and it was finally happening—I could finally let go—into the moonlit woods, into the golden light of the falling leaves.

When I left Andy that night, drunk as I was, I knew what I was doing. I wasn't riding home. I was riding *away.*

Hannah has her own reasons to want to get away.

Covering for Hannah, like she's asking me to do, isn't anything new. But if I don't cover for her—if I tell anyone what I know she's done, my world and her world—*everyone's world*—will crumble.

I pick up my phone and text Hannah.

Where r u?

When are you coming back?

I don't say I'll lie for her. But I don't say I won't.

TWO

THERE WERE SO many wasted nights at Robert Senna's, they all kind of blend into one, but the time we went to Alex's stands out as being particularly fucked up. I felt it from the start, even before we left Senna's for White Plains. I think I have a good instinct for knowing when something bad is coming my way; I can feel it, the way you can feel you're about to get a cold or the flu.

Early on, there was a fight between Senna and Chuck. As usual, Senna was messing with Chuck's head—baiting him. Hannah, Senna, and I were all on the couch by the window when Chuck walked up and banged on the downstairs door. Senna is always giving Chuck shit for not having manners—slamming the door to his truck, knocking too hard on the door of the house, or not knocking and walking in on Senna and Hannah when they're fooling around.

Senna shouted down, "Why the fuck you banging on my house?" Chuck gave him the finger, and Senna grabbed

Hannah's water bottle from the table, leaned out the open window and emptied it over Chuck's head. He got him pretty bad.

We nearly died laughing when we heard Chuck race up the stairs—*bang bang bang bang*. Then he burst in the room and threw his guitar case at Senna, missing him by a foot. Senna tackled him. Hannah and I screamed and jumped out of the way as Senna crashed around, trying to pin Chuck to the floor.

Chuck was furious—his wet T-shirt clung to his back, and his damp hair hung in his face as he grimaced and grunted, trying hopelessly to fend Senna off, and gain the advantage. Senna, though, seemed to be enjoying himself—exerting little effort, grinning and laughing as the two of them rolled around.

"Down boy," Senna said once he had him pinned, and Chuck stopped struggling. Then, after a tense moment, when it looked like they were about to start fighting all over again, Senna released him, and they sat up next to each other on the floor, Chuck breathing hard—Senna like a big, curly-headed bear, taking an occasional swipe at Chuck's shoulder, until Chuck finally lay sprawled on the floor, with his arms and legs spread like a hipster Jesus.

I thought to myself, *How did you choose, Hannah? How did you choose Senna the Psycho over wild, innocent Chuck?* And just for a moment, I let my eyes rest on Chuck, as his chest rose and fell with his still-heavy breathing. He had his shirt raised and his hand rested on a strip of tanned skin, and because Chuck is so thin, the waistband of his jeans gapped, exposing the elastic of his boxers.

It was Senna who snapped me out of it. "Yo, text your

boyfriend, Marcelle, and tell him to get his A-hole brother over here. I need Jonas to come now if we're setting this deal up tonight," Senna said. I stared at him blankly.

"Whose boyfriend?" I asked. I didn't like Senna referring to Andy as my boyfriend—it felt like he was mocking me. Andy and I had hooked up a few times over the summer, and a couple of nights before, we had ridden our bikes home from Senna's through the woods. We were both wasted, so we had stopped halfway and walked. What happened on that walk was vague. In the morning, I had scratches on my legs and leaves in my hair. I remember kissing Andy by the big white rock near Summit. I know things heated up between us, but I've lost most of the details. Drunk forgetting isn't like other kinds of forgetting— it's like your whole body forgets. Maybe that's what makes it so hard to ask Andy what he remembers. My brain wants to know, but my body wants to curl up in a corner.

I felt myself flush under Senna's gaze as I scrolled through my phone for Andy's number. I wanted to tell Senna to just text him himself, or text Jonas, but he knew he had me cornered, and cornering people is Senna's favorite form of entertainment. About a minute after I texted him, Andy and Jonas walked noisily up the stairs. When Andy glanced in my direction, I blushed, and silently cursed Senna. I'd had only one beer, not nearly enough.

Hannah sprang to her feet when she saw Jonas was carrying a bottle of Smirnoff Silver. "Thanks, Dad," she said. "You're the best." She took the bottle to the kitchen and mixed herself a lemonade and vodka in one of the grimy plastic cups the Sennas kept in the kitchenette. Senna's parents seem to have abandoned the garage apartment years ago, after his older brother, who had been living there, finally joined the army or navy or whatever.

"Marcelle, you in need of a shot?" Hannah offered.

"I'll take whatever you're having," I answered.

"I'm only mixing for my girl," Hannah announced. "Don't any of you guys get to thinking I'm your bitch." When she handed me my glass, Senna tried to snag it, but Hannah shoved him with her elbow and he frowned, feigning hurt, falling back on the sofa behind him.

"Elise says the worst thing you can do is train a guy wrong from the start. They get used to it, and then you spend your life in servitude," she said.

"Yeah," Senna said. "And who trains you? That I'd like to see."

"I train me," Hannah said, tossing her head. "And if you're smart, you won't go thinking you can change that."

Senna laughed. "That'd be like changing a cat to a dog, and who would want to do that?"

"Getting tired of babysitting here," Jonas said, leaning forward across the old trunk that served as a coffee table, chopping a small pile of white powder into lines. Senna lifted Hannah by the hips, and moved her to the seat next to him. She leaned back on the armrest, and put her bare feet in Senna's lap.

"Well, fucking get started, then," Senna said.

"I'm texting Alex now. See when he wants us," Hannah said. Jonas shook his head.

"You're crazier than I thought," Jonas said to Senna. "Letting your girlfriend loose with Alex."

"Shut up, man," Senna said. "Like you know."

About an hour after Jonas and Andy arrived, Senna demanded we leave. I'd had a couple of drinks, but I'd mostly been on my phone, hardly talking to anyone. Even on nights Andy and I hooked up, we started out slow, both of us wary.

"All right, drink up, kids," Senna said. "We've got to bounce."

"Hold on," Jonas said. "It's not cool to bring everyone over there. Five high school kids. That's no good." Jonas shook his head and crossed his arms, eyeing Senna. Jonas was cold sober, and Senna was close to it, but they both seemed to be spoiling for a fight.

"Fuck do you know?" Senna said. Somehow, Senna had managed to work things so that he and Hannah didn't need Jonas as a go-between with Alex, even though Alex was Jonas's friend. They'd met at the community college in White Plains, and then started working together at the tech company Alex supposedly started with money he made dealing coke.

"You can just give me your cash, if you think it's too many people. I'll drop by your place tomorrow," Senna said. Senna towered over Jonas, with a calm, almost-blank look, his fists loosely clenched.

"Fine," Jonas said disgustedly. "We got things settled already. More talk is just a way to fuck what we've got." But Senna seemed not to hear; he brushed past Jonas and bolted down the stairs, while everyone, including Jonas, followed him like a line of school kids.

"Let's go, woman," Senna said outside, as he grabbed Hannah by her tiny waist and lifted her into the cab of his truck. She shrieked and kicked, playing like she was being taken against her will, until Senna pushed her into the truck butt-first. Without a word, Chuck climbed in on the other side. I was left to go with Jonas and Andy, or not at all.

THREE

JONAS WAS UPSET about the argument with Senna, and a few times he nearly drove us off the road when he turned in his seat to yell at Andy. "Fucking Alex won't like this," he said. "Damn. I should've just brought those cokehead idiots, left you and your girl back home." I cringed in the backseat, both because Andy's brother didn't want me there, and because he seemed to know about the two of us. Then I caught Andy's eye in the rearview mirror, and he gave me a hesitant smile.

Senna, Hannah, and Chuck beat us to Alex's by about ten minutes, and when we walked in they were already talking to a twentysomething guy with a dark beard and weird tinted glasses, who I assumed must be Alex. The apartment was crowded with people around Jonas's age—people, I guessed, from the community college, and some even older guys who were maybe from Alex's tech company. I could see why Jonas hadn't wanted to bring us all. We were the youngest at the party by far, and I felt like people were staring.

Alex came up and gave Jonas a kind of man-hug, then he gave me a look over. Behind his tinted glasses, his squinty eyes were a watery blue. "Name?" he demanded.

"Marcelle," I said, and I put my hand out for him to shake, which I instantly regretted. He took it with mock seriousness.

"So nice to meet you, Marcelle. I think I'm already in love with those fiery curls of yours." He spoke in a fake, flirtatious voice. I blushed, and looked for a way to escape. "I got other business," he said. "But I'll keep an eye out for you."

"Thanks," I said awkwardly. Alex, I decided, was one of those guys who make it a thing to go after the girl who isn't the hot one.

Alex led Hannah, Senna, and Jonas toward a bedroom down the hall, but he stopped in front of the closed door, turned toward me, and winked. I looked away, but not before he caught my eye, and gave me a look full of meaning. I grabbed on to Andy's sleeve, afraid of losing him in the pressing crowd of the small apartment.

In the kitchen, people were playing beer pong at a table by the window, and others were passing around a small wooden pipe. There was a long-haired girl in a crop top with a tattoo across her abdomen that said *Child of Nature*, with a crescent moon and a sun above it. She was making her way around the room with a bottle of tequila and a stack of plastic glasses. The girl had a sort of lopsided face, but she had a graceful dancer's body.

Nature Girl sidled up next to Andy and me. "Bottoms up, baby!" she cried. I took a shot glass from her, wondering if she was calling me "baby" because she realized how young I was, or because she called everyone that. I drank my shot in one swallow, like you're supposed to, but Andy choked on his, drinking only half. The girl handed him a paper napkin, and patted him gently on the back. Then I put out my glass, and the girl poured me a second shot. Andy gave me a look of surprise, and I shrugged.

"That's what I call *girl power*," Nature Girl said.

"You're hard-core, Marci," Andy said. "Makes me look bad."

"Stop," I said, and slapped his arm. "I hardly drank at Senna's."

This wasn't really true. I'd had a couple strong drinks back at Senna's and a beer before Andy and Jonas got there. But I was unnerved by Alex and the older crowd around us, and I knew Andy and I had to talk, the sooner the better. If things continued being awkward between us, they might stay that way for good.

"You know, I wanted to say something about the other night—after we left Senna's," I started.

"Yeah, me too," he said. He looked down, playing with the thin leather bracelet on my wrist. "You were pretty wasted. I was too, but I thought maybe you were more fucked up," he said. I nodded. My heart raced. I needed a drink of water, but there was nothing on the table, except Andy's half-finished shot of tequila. I sipped at it. He bit his lip. I could see he had something serious to say. I took another sip of his tequila.

"Would you stop?" he said suddenly, grabbing my wrist.

"What?" I said.

"I'm trying to talk to you," he said, glancing at the drink in my hand.

"I'm sorry," I said. "I'll stop." I pushed the glass away.

"You're a great girl, Marci. At school, in class and everything," he started. "I really like you, but something happens . . ." He paused, and looked up at the ceiling. I was afraid of what he would say next. I felt like the pale tile floor of the kitchen suddenly wasn't entirely stable. I had trouble breathing.

"Are you okay?" he asked.

I shook my head. "I'll be right back," I said. "I've got to find a bathroom." Suddenly, it was like all the voices in the room had merged into one, and it sounded like insects buzzing. I thought if I could wash my face, I could get my head together and talk to Andy, and hear whatever was coming next. I knew which room Alex had led Hannah and Senna into, so I went in the opposite direction down the hall, and opened the first door I came to. It wasn't a bathroom, though, but a small room, like a study, with a couch against one wall, and the rest of the space filled with screens and tripods, camera equipment, and a couple of laptops. There was one window on the far wall, but it was covered with a black sheet. I took a step inside and was staring into the jumble of things, when someone came up from behind me, and shut the door.

It was Alex. "That ain't for you, honey," he said in his strange, soft voice. "Those are my toys. Should get a lock for this shit. All these kids walking around this place, someone's going to jack something." He stepped forward and pressed up against me, breathing in my ear. I could feel the roughness of his beard against my cheek.

"You looking for something, hon?" he whispered. I still had my back to him, and if I turned my head, my face would be much too close to his, so I stayed frozen in place. He pressed himself even closer, and I could feel him hard against me. He began to kiss my neck and stroke my hair. Then he put one hand firmly against the wall, blocking my way. He slid his other hand up my shirt and began to touch my breasts. He reached into my bra. My head throbbed. I felt dizzy, like my knees were about to buckle beneath me. I knew if I didn't do something soon, the situation would only get worse. But I couldn't think what to do. It was his house. I was drunk. I was afraid to make a scene.

Then he slid his hand down around my waist and started to pry deeper. I wanted to speak, say no, scream even, but somehow I couldn't get enough air into my lungs. Then suddenly, I heard Hannah call my name.

"Marcelle! Come on, we're out of here!"

I jerked around, and in surprise, Alex pulled back. I pushed past him, and we burst together through the door. Andy, Hannah, and the others were waiting in the front hall. They turned at the commotion. Alex darted into the kitchen, but it was obvious we'd been alone in that room, and that we'd been interrupted.

On our way down to the street, Andy walked ahead of me,

and didn't wait for me to catch up. Senna's truck was parked in the opposite direction, and I'd already lost sight of him and Hannah. I was terrified that Andy was mad, and that he and Jonas might leave without me. I started to walk faster, when I stumbled over an uneven corner of sidewalk. I went down hard on one knee, but got straight back up. I started to cry, but not aloud. I wiped my nose with the corner of my T-shirt, and tried to blink back my tears.

I wanted to explain everything to Andy—about the room, and what had happened with Alex, but we rode home in silence, and all I remember was that the windows were down, and I stopped crying, because there was something soothing about the warm, flower-scented air.

Jonas pulled up in front of my house, and to my surprise, Andy got out of the car and walked me down the stone path to the side door. I leaned on his arm so I wouldn't stumble in the dark, but I wasn't so drunk that I couldn't, finally, try to explain what had happened back at Alex's. "I didn't go in there with him," I whispered. "He followed me."

We stood under the outside light on the steps by the kitchen, near my mother's potted herbs and flowers. I was still shaken by what happened, but at least I'd tried to explain. Andy pushed my hair away from my face, and just stared at me for a minute, like he was thinking what he should say.

"I didn't think so," he said. "I just wanted to get out of there, and get you away from those fuckheads. Jonas has some real lowlife friends."

"Yeah, it was kind of scary," I said softly. I thought for a second what would have happened if Hannah hadn't called me when she did.

Andy squeezed my hand. "I don't want you to get hurt," he said. I knew what he meant. I was a drunk girl, who let fucked-up things happen to me. But I wanted to explain to Andy that sometimes for me being drunk wasn't like you'd expect. Inside, there was a part of me that wasn't fucked up at all. Inside, I was the normal me.

I felt the tears hot on my cheeks. I nodded silently. I could still feel Alex's breath on my neck. I could still hear his voice.

FOUR

IN THE SUMMER, I told myself it was a summer thing, and that I would stop in the fall. But when school started, I began to drink more than ever.

I snuck beer upstairs in my book bag, and dropped the empties out in the mornings on recycling days, hiding them in my closet until a Tuesday or Thursday. It was surprisingly easy. And it made being home alone in my room like a party, only better. I'd eat dinner with Mom and Dad, and then go upstairs to do homework and drink. I hid the beer bottles on the floor behind my desk in case either of them came in. I burned a mint-smelling candle that my mom always worried I'd forget to blow out.

On weekends, I told my parents I was staying in to study for my SATs. I told Hannah the same thing, and she gave me shit for being the world's biggest nerd. It hardly mattered, though. She was busy most nights with Senna, going to White Plains, and hanging out with Alex. She never asked me to come, not that I would have anyway.

I didn't know what Hannah and Senna were really up to, or even half of it, until Hannah filled me in one Saturday afternoon. She asked me to meet her at the Starbucks near the school. She seemed wired, too energetic for eleven in the morning, and I could tell she had something on her mind. I was hungover but I couldn't admit it, not even to Hannah, since I'd been by myself the night before, listening to music and drinking vodka in my room until I passed out on top of my covers with my shorts and flip-flops still on.

I stared at my coffee and waited for Hannah to say something. She sipped her tea and scanned the room. I realized she was checking to see if anyone was in hearing distance. Then, she leaned across the table and spoke so quietly I could hardly hear her. "Senna and I are meeting Alex tonight. Picking up some more stuff," she said. "I just hope these Waverly kids can keep quiet."

She had me nervous already. How could she be sure no one would snitch? Coke wasn't common in our town. It would definitely get around that people had some.

Hannah went on. "Alex said Senna and I should be able to clear a grand between us. Chuck has his own stash too. I'm saving mine for my car fund, or maybe just my fun fund," she said. In August, Hannah had gotten her nose pierced, and I still wasn't used to the look of the tiny gold dragonfly stud she wore. With the gold flecks in her eyes, the golden ends of her hair, and the dragonfly, there was something unsettling about her appearance—like she wasn't a real person, but like a painting or a photograph.

"What are you looking at?" Hannah snapped. I was jarred; I hadn't realized I'd been staring.

I sipped my coffee and tried to think what to say. "Aren't you scared?" I finally asked. "It's not like it's weed. You guys could get busted, like Ellen what's-her-name." Ellen was a senior girl who'd suddenly disappeared last January. The story was that she was selling her Ritalin to a bunch of kids who got caught snorting it in the town library during midterms and ratted her out.

Hannah drank her tea, eyed me slyly, and said, "I was talking to Alex about it, and you know what he said? He said 'You're so pretty. No one ever wants to rat on the pretty girl.'" Hannah's uncombed hair fell across her face.

I hesitated. "I think that's just the kind of thing a guy like Alex says," I ventured. "But you know I have beef with him."

Hannah ignored my comment. "We can make a grand or two in one month, without even working. How much did you make at that day camp over the summer?"

"Six hundred," I mumbled. I could see where she was going.

"Yeah, and your parents will probably buy you a car," Hannah said. "Elise is making me choose—and I chose singing lessons." She leaned back in her chair, as though she had made her point.

"And where are you going to tell her you got this car money?" I asked.

Hannah looked down at her hands. "Elise won't ask where the money came from. Anyway, I haven't even gotten my permit yet. She can't find the time to take me, she says. Too many paintings to finish for her November show."

Hannah's plan made a sick sort of sense. She has a great voice, and her mom isn't like my parents. She doesn't pry into Hannah's business. She's too busy with her painting and her gallery in the city.

"I guess you know what you're doing," I said, and Hannah nodded.

"It's no big deal," Hannah said. "Literally—not a big deal. Chuck is figuring out the numbers, and exactly what we'll cut it with. Mr. Chemistry, you know. And Senna is making a list of kids he thinks are all right—kids who won't spread it all over town."

"Sounds like easy money," I said. "And it'll probably be done with fast." I was embarrassed that I seemed to be more worried than she was.

"Probably sell it all in a weekend," Hannah said. "It's only going to be about fifteen or twenty grams. I don't even need to put up any cash." She stopped herself, took a sip of tea, and then went on. "Maybe we need thirty kids to sell to, reliable kids. Tell me if you can think of anyone who might want some, who isn't a talker. Don't text. Give me any names in person. Senna and I are going to cut it next week—cutting it to shit, so it's practically nothing. You want to give the good stuff a try, on me?" Hannah winked. I knew she knew what I'd say.

"No way," I shook my head. "When I did that one line at your house, I wanted to jump out the window. Coke makes me even more nervous than I already am." I grimaced. "It's a nightmare. I'm after the dream."

Hannah laughed. "You were bugging," she said. "I never saw such a waste of a good buzz. Anyway, it'd keep you from getting so drunk, and getting into trouble. Like with Alex."

I stared at her. "Hannah," I said, "why would you even say that? He *followed* me in there. *He* was the trouble."

Hannah looked puzzled. "How was I supposed to know? Tell me what happened."

I sighed. Somehow, it didn't seem worth the effort to explain to Hannah about that night. It was over. Alex was an asshole. Hannah had to know that. Maybe there was nothing to talk about, except why Hannah hung out with him so much when she knew I hated him. "Anyway, what's the deal with him? What does he actually do?" I asked.

Hannah hesitated, and got a vague look on her face. "I don't know everything about his tech company. But he's fronting me my half of the blow. Senna had about five hundred left from some money his grandparents gave him last year, but I had nothing, as usual, so Alex asked me to do some modeling for him." She faltered and blushed. It wasn't like Hannah to get embarrassed.

"Actual modeling, like for stores . . . ?" I trailed off.

"Well, not exactly," she said, laughing and looking around at the tables close to us. "I'll tell you later. It's kind of bad," she said. "But not, you know, *insane*."

"'Not insane,'" I repeated. "That's good. That sounds great." I couldn't help being sarcastic. It was one of the few times I even questioned what Hannah was doing.

"I swear, Marcelle, I'll tell you more. But you have to promise on your life you won't tell anyone, ever, not even Andy." She leaned across the table. "*Promise*," she repeated.

"I promise," I said. Then I added, "Anyway, Andy and I are hardly seeing each other." But Hannah didn't respond. She was done confiding. It would be weeks before Hannah told me more.

She picked up her bag and got up to leave. "I need to meet Senna," she said. "We're going over some songs I want to learn. I'm getting an audition with that teacher I told you about at the Performing Arts Center. It's in a few weeks. Most of the kids she works with have been singing for years. I've got to sound hot."

I followed her out into the bright sun of the parking lot as she put her headphones on and walked away. She had asked me to meet her so I'd give her names of kids who would make good customers. It was the last thing I wanted to do—send people I knew to Hannah to get fucked up, and so she could get in even deeper with Alex.

I unlocked my bike from the bike rack and wheeled it to the sidewalk. I thought about texting Andy to see if he wanted to get lunch at the diner, or take a walk by the water, but I knew I wouldn't. It was too risky. If he said no, I'd still have to see him Monday in English. He'd told me the week before he liked my essay about being an only child. I'd written about how I learned as a little kid to make up stories, and think about myself as a character in a book, so I wouldn't feel so lonely.

It's the kind of thing teachers love. But it wasn't really true. It wasn't about me, but more like the girl I wished I was. I made up stories, that was the true part—but they were always about lonely little girls—orphans and sad, ragged runaways—lost kids, or kids who had never had a home.

FIVE

MAYBE I'M LOSING my mind.

I know I could find a Benadryl somewhere in the house, and that if I took one, I could fall blissfully asleep. But I know I have to resist. Benadryl, NyQuil, anything that knocks you out, is considered a banned substance at the Center. I know I can't face Group tomorrow if I slip. The thought of sitting in Group and having to either lie or confess is the only thing that keeps me from rummaging through my closet. I can't become the loser James and Cyndi already think I am.

I pace, pick up my phone, and put it back on the bed. It's been almost two hours since I heard from Hannah, since the "undeliverable" alert popped up when I texted her back. The rational part of me knows there's no reason to panic. But I can't help it. My crash has made me wary. I can't help thinking that Hannah's crash is coming too.

The night of my Death Wish crash, it was hot and humid, and Hannah had wanted to swim. It was risky to go to the quarry near Senna's when it was still light, and people might be out walking their dogs, but by about five it seemed okay.

I remember Hannah on the highest rock, frozen on a slab of gray stone, the low sun lighting the back of her head, so her hair was slightly aglow—I remember thinking, *No, don't.* Andy stood next to me, and he grabbed my hand when she dove.

Oh Jesus, oh Jesus. Andy turned away. Chuck, pale and thin, stood on the rocks, the next to jump, and Senna leaned against the truck smoking, like he'd seen this movie before.

Hannah climbed out of the water in just her bra and panties. She flipped her hair back and wrung it out with both hands. Senna fished a towel out of the back of his pickup. No one paid any attention to Chuck. He must have hit bottom hard, although he made it out okay, climbing over the sharp rocks, cupping his nose. He looked like a boxer, bloody-faced, his lip already swollen. Hannah handed him the wet towel off her shoulders and climbed into her own cutoffs.

"You okay?" Andy asked. Chuck nodded, and Hannah put her arm around his slender waist. You could feel Senna's silent fury as the three of them climbed into the cab of Senna's truck.

"You kids had enough fun yet?" Jonas said, shaking his head.

We all ended up back at Senna's. Hannah called Alex, and he came over with some blow. The joke was that doing some bumps would help numb Chuck's face. Hannah and Senna had already sold their first stash, or at least what was left of it that they hadn't done themselves.

"It's good medicine, Chuckles," Hannah said as she chopped lines on an old mirror. Chuck's nose was swollen, and he had dark circles under his eyes. Bruised and helpless, he followed her every move.

"What a dumbfuck," Senna said, shaking his head. Alex and Jonas laughed with Senna over Chuck's attempt to follow Hannah into the quarry.

"You're just too fat to swim, *Robby*," Chuck said. "Fat piece of shit." Senna shot Chuck a murderous look.

"Come on, kids," Alex said, "Let's play nice." Hannah handed Chuck the mirror first, and it was clear Senna was still annoyed that Hannah was nursing Chuck.

"Man," Senna said. "You're lucky I'm a patient guy. You try to squeeze on my girl, you do my drugs, then you call me names?" Senna shook his head menacingly.

Andy and I hung back in the kitchen, away from Alex and the whole tense scene. Occasionally, I felt Alex's gaze on me, but he kept his distance in the living room.

I'd had a beer over at the quarry, but for me one beer had zero effect, and I was feeling jumpy with Alex around, so I hit the vodka hard. Andy seemed to get my mood. He watched me do two shots in a row without saying a word. Then he poured himself a shot, drank it, and poured another for each of us. "Cheers," he said. I took a step closer to him, so we were almost touching—hoping he'd put his arm around me, or even kiss me.

That's when he turned cold.

"I can't do this, Marci," he said softly.

"Do what?" I asked.

"You get too drunk," he said. "I tried to tell you that night after Alex's. If we're going to get that fucked up together, we can't—I can't, you know, hook up. I can't be that guy. I don't want it to be like it was over the summer." He took a couple of steps away, and leaned against the greasy-looking green-and-black kitchen counter.

"You mean because of the night in the woods?" I asked. Andy stared at me, his usually spiky hair starting to droop over one eye. He looked, for a second, like a slightly older version of the twelve-year-old Andy I remembered from middle school, the kid who Ms. Billings made cry when he forgot his home-work, the kid who hated to share anything he'd written, even if he'd gotten the best grade in class. He blinked a few times, and looked at the ceiling.

"Yeah," he continued. Then he lowered his voice. "I don't want something bad to happen," he said. "You were really fucked up that night. We both were. But I don't want it to be like I took advantage of you. I don't want to do something and then wish we didn't."

I felt a lump in my throat, but I choked back the tears. Andy watched me silently as I turned my head away, and tilted back two or three more shots. If he wanted me to choose between him and drinking, I'd show him which I was more into. Anyway, how could I be sure Andy liked me at all—maybe his saying I got too drunk was just an excuse not to hook up?

Either way, it wasn't fair he got to decide.

When I left that night, I heard Andy behind me, calling my name. But I had my bike with me, and I rode away too quickly for him to catch up on foot. I cried in the dark with the wind in my face. I cried and rode faster and faster. I rode straight into the darkness of the Death Wish path. Then the clouds must have cleared, or the moon came up over the hill; a faint light shone deeper in the woods. I rode toward that light, although I could barely see the path in front of me.

This is the story I told in Group on Friday. Cyndi congratulated me. She said, "You were crushed by your crush. That's such a great start!"

"Andy actually sounds like your only friend," James added.

I cried a little when I finished talking. I didn't say what I thought—which is that I wished Andy didn't have to be so good. It would be easier if he were bad like me, if he would let things happen however they happened, even if that meant no one was in control.

The so-called "modeling" Hannah was doing for Alex was supposed to be a one-time thing, so Hannah and Senna could get twice as much coke from Alex. Senna kept saying he didn't want his girlfriend to become some kind of *webcam whore*. Hannah complained about it one day when we met for lunch at the diner—how jealous Senna was of Alex, and even of the guys who paid to watch her. "In a way it's ridiculous," she said. "In another way, it's sad. But really it's kind of like nothing. It's boring, unless I try to entertain myself, and think about it like a movie, and like I'm some kind of star." She made it sound almost like a joke, or something anyone would do.

Hannah didn't ask me about my life, or how I was doing at the Center, and it made me think about what the kids there all say about friendship, and having friends who do drugs and fuck up. They say everyone has *that* friend, the one who you'll follow all the way down.

SIX

MY MOM OPENS my door halfway, peeks in, then stands in the doorway in her baby-blue bathrobe and bare feet. "I'm too tired for this, kiddo," she says. Her voice is deep and rough-sounding.

"I just got a call from Elise Scott, looking for Hannah. Do you have any idea where she is? Elise seemed to think she was here studying. What is this nonsense, Marcelle?"

A part of me wants to spill everything, to tell my mother about the text Hannah sent hours ago, and how I've heard nothing since. How odd it is. How Hannah never turns her phone off. But I can't. Hannah's lie tonight is a loose thread, and there are too many ways that Hannah's life and mine are woven together.

"I have no clue," I say. I pull my covers up to my neck, and try to sound sincere.

"She was in town earlier, and said she wanted to come by,

but I told her I couldn't hang out. She said she'd walk over to Senna's instead. She probably fell asleep there." I yawn. Everything I say is plausible.

"I guess it isn't our problem if Hannah doesn't tell her mother where she goes," Mom says. "But this gives me pause, Marcelle. The fact that Elise Scott is completely in the dark about where Hannah is on a school night does not sit well with me."

"What is it, Jude?" Dad calls from the bedroom. Shit. The last thing I need is both my parents on my back about where Hannah is. I don't need to get busted on the smallest of lies, covering for Hannah when I don't even know myself what the fuck she's doing.

"It's fine, Jim. Just something with Hannah. Marcelle says it's nothing."

"I've got to get some sleep, Mom," I say. I try to sound nonchalant. Mom limps toward my bed. Her knee arthritis has been acting up, which happens, she says, when she's stressed. She leans down to kiss my forehead, a thing she hasn't done in years. I want to jerk away, but I let her kiss me, then inspect the rough skin where the stitches were.

"I'm glad we got that plastic surgeon, Marcelle," Mom says. "I don't think you'll have much of a scar."

Mom and I look at each other for an awkward moment. I feel like I'm about seven, with my Mom tucking me in. She stands up and pulls her bathrobe close to her chest. "Good night, sweetheart," she says. "I'll pick you up right at three tomorrow. Please don't make me wait. I have a call."

33

"No problem," I say, and roll over. For half a second I thought maybe Mom had forgiven me for being such a fuck-up, but no. She had to get that last dig in about how her whole life has been thrown into chaos because she has to work from home and drive me back and forth to the Center every day.

Mom shuts the door, and I close my eyes. I need rest, but my mind is racing. There are facts that add up to something, I tell myself.

When Hannah texted for me to cover for her, I figured she was with Alex, and just didn't want Senna to know. But it's strange for her to stay out so late on a Sunday, when she knows her mom will start looking for her. What kind of story did she expect me to tell?

I try not to think about tomorrow, or tomorrow night, or all the endless days and nights I have to get through without drinking a single drink. It's like holding on to a rock in a high-up place, and not being afraid of falling so much as having to hold on, because I know how it will feel when I fall. I know that if I drank, even just a couple of beers, that I could let go, let go of trying to be what I'm supposed to be—to my parents; at Group—I'd fall, and I know the fall would be soft, and the darkness would welcome me, because drinking is always like that—it's oblivion—it's bottomless, an actual pit sometimes, but it also feels just like home.

SEVEN

"**SPEAK, MARCELLE. GIVE** it up." I'm confused. Senna is on the attack and Hannah is nowhere to be seen. It's Monday morning and the bell is about to ring. Senna's been looking for Hannah since before she texted me last night, and he seems to think I know more than I do.

"She was just checking up on me," I say. "Making sure my parents hadn't shipped me off somewhere."

Senna shoves his big, pale face in front of mine. I shrug and look at my feet. Apparently Hannah hasn't answered any of his texts or calls since yesterday afternoon. "I went everywhere I could think last night—Harbor Park, down by the marina, even walked over to the quarry, but I didn't see anyone." Senna blinks his narrow eyes rapidly and shakes his hair off his forehead, as he scans the school parking lot for some sign of Hannah.

"Then, I drove all the way the fuck over to White Plains and got Alex up," he continues. "He and that freak roommate of his came to the door carrying. Guy holding a baseball bat. Alex with a big-ass knife. Alex was like, 'What the fuck do I know about some little girl?'" Senna pauses, takes a deep breath, and turns to Andy. "Where's your bro, anyway? Maybe he has something the fuck to say."

"I saw him last night. He came by for dinner. My parents are pissed because he was supposed to get his applications in for spring semester and he's still blowing it off. It was not a pleasant evening at my abode," Andy said. On the rare occasions Andy and I talk about anything personal, it's the same—Andy's parents fighting either with or about Jonas.

"Let me see that text she sent you," Senna says, putting his meaty hand out for my phone. I shoot Andy a look. "I deleted it," I say. "My parents take my phone away at night. I delete pretty much everything." This is a lie, but I can't let Senna see that Hannah was avoiding him.

Senna narrows his eyes. I shiver. I know Senna suspects something, but nothing good can come of admitting that Hannah wanted me to lie. Senna's story about going to Alex's freaks me out even more. Like Senna, I suspected Alex was somehow involved in whatever Hannah was up to last night. Was Alex lying? Did he come to the door armed with a knife because Hannah was there, and he knew her boyfriend would come looking for her? A thousand thoughts run through my mind.

First bell has rung, but all three of us stay put, under the big oak, as kids start to move toward the school entrance. Senna sighs and kicks at a tree root. If only Hannah would show up. She sometimes comes late, but I know she has Photography first today, a class she hates to miss. Senna was out half the night looking for Hannah, and Hannah *never* got in touch with him. She asked me to cover for her, but never explained why. It's like she didn't want to be found, not just for a few hours, but for *the entire night*.

Lost in my own swirling thoughts, I don't notice Chuck until he's standing right next to me. His eyes are red and puffy. "You okay?" I ask, but he acts like I'm not there, and directs his attention toward Senna.

"What's up?" he says. But Senna is too preoccupied with Hannah to respond.

"Maybe she's at her dad's," I say. "He's out of the country a lot. She could have just wanted a break, get out of town for a bit."

Senna eyes me suspiciously. "Why would she want to get away? For what?"

I shrug.

"You're a big fucking help, Marcelle," Senna says sneeringly. To my surprise, he's getting teary.

"Easy," Andy interrupts. "What's Marci got to do with any-thing?" I feel myself flush when Andy comes to my defense.

"What the fuck are you guys talking about?" Chuck asks.

"Hannah's kind of gone," Andy says. "Since last night. I bet she's at her dad's, like Marci says. Maybe she got in a fight with her mom and took off."

"She'd tell me that," Senna says. "I saw her in the morning, yesterday. She came by, then left at, like, noon. She said she was going home. She had an audition with some lady in White Plains for singing classes today. She wanted to practice by herself and nail the vocal."

"The audition is this afternoon," I say. "She won't blow that off."

"No, uh-uh," Chuck adds. "The three of us practiced that one song all last week."

"That's it," Senna says, shaking his head. "She blows this audition off and there's no way I'm listening to you mangle a pulse one more time, Glasser."

"Forget you," Chuck says. "I'm not even responding to that shit."

It's late and Andy and I have English, but I'm too freaked out to leave the tree, or to walk away from Senna and Chuck and their stupid bickering.

"This is majorly messing with my head," I say. Andy looks solemn, and I think how much he has to deal with having that fuck-up Jonas for a brother, and two idiots like Chuck and Senna as his best friends.

"Yeah, well," Senna says. "Maybe you should have asked what the fuck was up with her last night, Marcelle." He turns his head and hisses, *"Bitch."* It's unclear whether this is directed at me or Hannah.

"Shit," Andy says. "We've got to stay cool, and think what's logical here." People stream into the building and the four of us drift that way too. I scan the front parking lot, yet again, for any sign of Hannah. With each step I take, I feel an increasing sense of dread, a chill that spreads throughout my body. The guys and I all pause at the glass doors. I'm grateful when Senna and Chuck take a left toward the math building, and Andy and I go right.

"What do you think?" Andy asks. He shoots me a look, his eyes wide and dark, so dark you can barely see the pupils. I want to ask him what *he* thinks—about Hannah, about us, but I'm not feeling very brave.

Everyone calls the path through the wooded part of our town the Death Wish path, because of a story from the nineties. People say that some girl was found out there in the woods with her neck slashed; they say anyone who goes there at night must have a death wish. But I didn't want to die that night. I was afraid of what would happen if Andy and I were never anything real, and Hannah was always off with Senna and Alex, and I was left alone for the rest of high school. Andy said he "couldn't be that guy." He didn't want to get with me when I was drunk. I know I should feel good about that, like Cyndi and James say. But it also scares me. I think once a guy gets turned off by you, it's kind of like a switch that might never go back on.

I pause at the door to Bartow's classroom. "A part of me doesn't want to think about Hannah at all," I say. "I have enough to worry about."

"Yeah," Andy says. "That makes sense. You need to focus on you."

I blush. "You sound like my dad," I say. Andy shrugs, and opens the classroom door.

"I just think Hannah can take care of herself."

Andy and I spend most of English listening to Ms. Bartow lecture us about basic punctuation rules, and then we get about five minutes to peer edit each other's "This I Believe" essays. We exchange papers and he, annoyingly, finds multiple errors in my first paragraph.

Sitting next to Andy, and thinking about Hannah, I can hardly concentrate. My heart beats too fast and too hard. I watch the clock and wonder if Hannah has come to school yet. My phone is on silent. I think ahead to the end of class, when I can check to see if she texted me. I want to believe that Andy is right—Hannah *can* take care of herself. But there's another part of me that thinks that's wrong. It's the opposite. She just thinks she can, no matter what kind of fucked-up situation she gets herself into.

I can't concentrate on Andy's paper, and instead of making editorial comments I decide to take a chance and type right into his document: *She told me to lie to Senna.*

I wait for his response. Senna is his friend. But I need to know if I can trust Andy—if he'll keep this secret from Senna and help me find out where Hannah went.

When we pass each other back our iPads, Andy has erased my note. At 9:05, we're dismissed. Andy walks out ahead of me. In the hallway, he pauses. "We should talk," he says.

"I'm going to Mr. Figeroa at lunch," I say. I need to make up a chem lab from when I was out. "Then Mom gets me at three. Then I have jail until six," I say.

Andy reaches over and brushes an old brown leaf off my book bag. This is the first flirty gesture he has made in weeks. "How about later?" he asks.

"I'm going to Michiko Sakuna's. You know, the lady who lives in that modern house off Summit?" Andy nods. "My parents are making me do chores for her to thank her for saving my life," I say. "I'll be there around six fifteen to six thirty or so. I can call you from there. I'll be alone."

Michiko Sakuna is the neighbor whose car I landed under, and who called the cops the night of my accident. I used to take care of her pets back in middle school, when she and her son went away. My parents wanted me to pay her back for her trouble, and for leaving a pond of blood in the middle of her driveway where I fell. For the next few months, I'm committed to feeding her pets every night, since she usually doesn't get home from work until after eight. It's a joke of a job, but I like her and her house.

"Did you see my note?" I ask, dropping my voice to a whisper.

Andy nods. "If she doesn't show this afternoon for that audition, I think you should tell someone." I feel my throat tighten. Andy looks at the floor, then back at me. He clears his throat. "It's not just Hannah," he says. "Jonas is messed up, too. Doing coke all the time. He's always over at Alex's. But this whole tech company, you know what it is, don't you? She told you what they're doing, right?"

Hannah made me promise on my life not to say anything to Andy, but it turns out he knows? I nod. "Yeah, she told me. I wasn't sure if anyone other than Senna knew. I don't understand how she could be involved with Alex. I just don't get it," I say.

Andy shakes his head. "Jonas told me a few weeks ago. He was really jacked up and couldn't stop talking. He said he needs to get away. Get away from Alex. I hope he can. I hope he can get his shit together, before my dad gets a fucking heart attack."

The hallway has filled with people, and Andy and I are getting pushed closer and closer together, until our shoulders touch. "Shit," he says. "I've got to go. Let me know what happens—if she texts you or anything, okay? Call me from Michiko's. I'll see if I can find out anything from Jonas." He gives the end of my braid a tug, and joins the throng of kids headed toward the science wing. Usually Andy talks to everyone, but as I watch him walk through the crowd with his hood up and his head down, everyone seems to move out of his way.

EIGHT

MOM PICKS ME up at three, and we're quiet for most of the ride to the Center. She doesn't ask me about whether Hannah showed up at school today. I assume she has other things on her mind, and I don't say anything about it either. At a red light on Weaver Street, I ask about her knee. She stretches her leg out. "Much improved. I'll be back at spin class by tomorrow," she says.

When the light turns green, she accelerates in her slow, steady way, and without looking at me she says, "You know, Marcelle, I love you and want the best for you. I'm concerned, though. I'm concerned this place—the Center—isn't giving you enough structure. You're still in with this same group at school, and it makes me think that you aren't totally committed to . . . getting better." She sighs. "I just want you to be healthy. Healthy and happy."

I don't say anything for a minute. My chest feels tight. I

want to break down and cry, and confess that I'm worried, really worried, about Hannah. After first period, my day was a blur. I kept calling Hannah, and getting her stupid voicemail. I looked for her between classes in the crammed hallways. I searched for her in the cafeteria during my free period, and then back at the tree at lunch. The guys and I ate on the hill in near silence. I sipped at my Styrofoam-cup-tasting cafeteria tea, and broke off pieces of a bagel that was too chewy and too dry.

At one point, Chuck kicked the ground and said, "Senna or Marcelle, maybe one of you should call Elise?" Senna shook his head. "Can't," he said. "Elise hates me. Thinks *I'm* a bad influence on *Hannah*." As if it made no sense at all that Elise Scott would consider Senna anything but a model boyfriend. The truth is it goes both ways—Senna and Hannah feed off each other.

"Maybe I'll call when I get home," I said, although I wasn't sure I meant this. What, exactly, would I say to Elise? I had tried to cover for Hannah, like Hannah asked. It hadn't done much good, but now I was stuck with having lied.

"I'll look for her after sixth period," Senna said. Senna and Chuck are the only ones of us who drive to school. I wanted to ask him where he planned to look, but I kept my mouth shut. I had to assume it involved him going back to Alex's place.

"Let me know when you go," Andy said. "I can skip soccer." But Senna didn't answer him, just chewed on a piece of grass, staring at nothing.

I can't tell Mom any of this—how all the guys are just as upset as I am.

If Mom hears about Hannah skipping school, she'll only get more freaked out. I don't need the pressure.

"They say that I have to take responsibility for my own choices," I say. "That's what they're teaching me here. I can't expect other people, even you and Dad, to solve my problems. But you're both always around. It's making me crazy the way you guys watch my every move."

We sit in the Center parking lot. Mom's face reddens, and she shuts her eyes; she's struggling to hold it together.

"I guess I really don't know what makes you happy, or what you think will give you a good life in the future. But I want to know. I want to be able to help you move forward without being overbearing. I just know you need to feel okay without needing alcohol," she says.

I sigh. There's so much to say and also nothing to say. Drinking did make me feel okay, and even better than that—happy and free—at least while I was doing it. In the mornings I always felt the opposite—like I was living in a kind of hole, and like no one could understand me. But I can't admit any of that to Mom. She's different from me. She's always got a plan, or a plan for a plan—like everything in life is one more problem that you can solve if you're smart enough. Even things like birthdays or holidays are things she wants to "do right." *Let's do Christmas right this year. Let's do summer right.* Then she starts planning— where we'll go, what we'll eat, like those are the only things that matter, and like she's never been bored or lonely or in a bad mood for no real reason. Mom's not the kind of person who can understand how trapped I feel in my own head.

I stall, take a long drink out of my water bottle, trying to calm my nerves. "I don't know, Mom. I don't know what could make me happy, other than getting really drunk. I wish I did, though." I half cry and half yell as I hop from the car and head across the parking lot with my head down, tears streaming across my face.

Mom backs out of her parking space and slams on the breaks, so I either have to walk around the car or talk to her. I want to keep walking, but I can't face her later if I do. I stop and turn, but glance toward the building, to let her know she's making me late.

"We aren't yellers," Mom says firmly, through her open window. "We talk. We always have. It's no different now, Marcelle. There isn't anything you can't tell us. I promise you that."

"I know," I say quietly. "I'm sorry." There isn't anything to fight about. What she says just isn't true. I can't tell Mom about Hannah, or Alex, or even about me and Andy, and how things were with us over the summer. I don't want her to know my secrets. I can feel her eyes on me, and all I want in the world is for her to leave.

If I could somehow vanish before reaching the entryway to the drab brick building in front of me, I would. But I arrive at the heavy metal door, pull it open, and walk down the gray carpeted stairs into the lower level of the building, as I have every weekday for the last two weeks. I sign in, pass the therapists' offices, wave hello to my therapist, Kevin, even though he's looking the other way, and put my stuff in the unmarked cubby Cyndi assigned me my first day here. I feel both conspicuous and invisible as I take my seat at the Group table. I am the last person to arrive, but no one acknowledges me.

NINE

EVERYONE IS FOCUSED on James. "Let's get started," James says. "We'll start with Cyndi's book, then we'll see what kind of time we have left to do the regular rotation." James leans against the table in his white oxford button-down, hands folded in front of him, hair messily flopped over one eye and buzz cut on both sides, in a mod, skater-boy fashion. James is a senior from Mount Kisco, a woodsy town about forty minutes north. None of the kids from my Peer Support Group for New Living go to school here in Waverly, which is a blessing, especially now. If I had to go to Group with someone who knew Hannah, I don't know what I'd do. Group is supposed to be confidential, but as I look around the table, I'm still not sure who I trust.

As James reaches for his meeting notes, the cuff of his shirt rides up just high enough to reveal the faded, purplish track marks that dot his delicate wrist. It's difficult to believe that only eight months ago James was a full-on junkie; hard to imagine him as anything other than a Group leader, a sober golden boy, with intense blue eyes that I can't help feeling see right through me.

I absentmindedly finger the rough spot on my chin. One day, it'll fade completely and everyone will forget about my Death Wish crash and I'll be a normal girl. Maybe the same will be true of Hannah. She could turn up in a half hour, or an hour, or at midnight tonight. She could get sober, or at least quit blow, quit Alex, quit all her shit, and reschedule her audition. Senior year, Hannah might be the star of the school musical, or in a legit band. Who knows?

Cyndi, our other Group leader, is sober for six months today, so this is her six-month meeting. At the Center, being sober at in-patient rehab, like where Cyndi spent eight weeks of her life, doesn't even count. We count only voluntary sobriety, meaning only the months we stay sober while living our real lives—at home with our families, going to school, being around people who drink and do whatever they want. Only James has a longer run of sobriety. I try to focus on Cyndi. I want to feel happy for her and to think that someday that could be me, but today this possibility feels remote. If Hannah doesn't show up tonight, what will I do tomorrow? My lie was a small one. All I said was that Hannah had gone to Senna's when she hadn't. But if Hannah is actually missing, like really missing, any lie might seem like a big deal.

Cyndi stands in the front of the room in her black leggings, a black tank, and Doc Martens. There's a dress code at the Center, so she wears a red-and-black flannel on top, but only pulled on halfway, leaving her bony shoulders exposed. Cyndi has chosen to make a scrapbook that includes pictures of her from her user days, and then some pictures and diary entries from when she got sober. I've seen a few other sixth-month books on a shelf in Kevin's office, and all of them have at least one picture from around intake. We're supposed to look at our addict selves with love and self-forgiveness, not shame. But it seems, at least to me, like Cyndi has gone overboard in including dozens of pictures from when she was using. I feel uncomfortable staring as Cyndi places her bound scrapbook on its edge, so we can take in the eight-by-eleven-inch print of Cyndi at eighty-five pounds, the week she lived on the streets in Brooklyn with her boyfriend, a guy almost ten years older than her, who she met one afternoon when her father hired him to clean out the underbrush near the brook in the back of their Pocantico mansion. Cyndi lives in one of the oldest corners of lower Westchester, where the houses don't have yards behind them, they have meadows and pools, greenhouses, and enormous three- and four-car garages. There's one picture Cyndi shows with an orchard in the background with peaches on the trees. She says "This was an acid day" as she flips the page.

"Here's Chris and me together," she says, showing an image of herself, looking very thin in a white tank with no bra, leaning on a tall guy in a grassy field. Cyndi faces the camera, her mouth wide open in a moment of hilarity. Chris looks sidelong at the lens and his eyes have a shiftiness I recognize. He's one of those guys, like Senna, who you can't read. You look in their eyes and you just notice what isn't there.

"This is at our place. Chris was doing yard work for us. That's how we met. Dad owed Chris's uncle a fave. They're buddies from Yale. But then Chris is Chris and he repaid him by hitting on me. I was hanging out by the pool with my friend Jess, drinking gin and tonics. One thing led to another." She sighs and flips the page

Cyndi has been back in school for two months, but she's still trying to fit in. She's a pretty girl with high cheekbones and full lips, or she would be if she hadn't left pretty behind for all-out edgy, with her thick black eyeliner, nose ring, and her two visible tattoos—the large butterfly behind her ear, and the snake that wraps hissingly around her middle finger. I wonder if Cyndi went to Waverly, if she'd be friends with my friends, or at least Senna, Chuck, and Hannah.

Cyndi finishes her talk, and moves from the hard-core past to the sober present. "Sad thing is," she says, "I was really happy with Chris in the beginning. Looking at these pictures is hard. I realize now, I never saw where I was headed. I was stoked all the time. So was Chris. It didn't feel like fucking up. It felt like a really powerful love. I know that's a user thing—confusing getting high with getting the love you want . . ." She trails off, wipes her eyes, smudging her eyeliner. "I know now Chris didn't love me. He used me. I know I used him, too. That's all we could do, because that's what users do."

There's a momentary silence as Cyndi pulls herself together. Then Martin says, "I hear you, girl. I hear that loud and clear. Be a user and get yourself used. That's what I say." Martin half closes his eyes and nods at Cyndi, willing her to go on. Cyndi stands up straighter.

She breathes deeply. "I really despise school," she says. "Everyone I *was* friends with is a user. Everyone else thinks I'm a freak. So it sucks. Every day these girls come up to me and ask me if I'm new in town, even though I went to five years of school with these bitches. It's a game to them to act like they don't remember me." She pauses and takes a breath. It's like the pause of a cigarette smoker without the drag. "But heads up!" she suddenly shouts. "This bitch is sober six months! Doing it for myself and no one else! I've got my Sixer!" She suddenly steps up on her chair with her six-month book over her head and takes a bow. Martin jumps to his feet and claps and whistles through his teeth.

I wish my phone were not back in my cubby, but there are no cell phones allowed in the Group room. I want to check my messages before Group ends. If I got just one text from Hannah, or from somebody who has seen Hannah, I won't have to say anything to anyone.

Martin walks slowly around the table and helps Cyndi down from her chair. To my surprise, she buries her face in his chest and he strokes her back. This show of affection unnerves me. In my mind, James and Cyndi are the "couple" of the Group, even though sexual contact between any of us is strictly forbidden.

Martin, unlike Cyndi, still seems unsure of himself, like every day sober takes all of his effort. I thought Martin could be the one person in Group who might have some sympathy for my continuing to fuck up. Everyone knows about the Death Wish night, but I haven't said much more in Group, aside from fessing up to all the beer and vodka I stole from Mom and Dad. It's hard to see a way forward for me, unless I tell them all about Hannah. If Elise Scott has called the police, and I don't confess to covering for Hannah, my parents will never understand. I can't tell them the whole web of lies—about Alex, the coke, or the webcam business. But I can at least come clean about last night.

I assume now that Cyndi is done, the Group will move on. As the silence in the room persists, I feel almost ready to bring the Group's attention to myself. Beads of sweat break out on my forehead. My heart beats hard in my chest as I clear my throat to speak. But just as I'm about to raise my hand, Ali speaks up.

"I have feedback for Cyndi on her six-monther," he says. Everyone turns to Ali. I feel my heart drop like a weight. "I think, Cyndi, when you look for a group of people to hang with at school now, you're thinking like a junkie. You want to be one of *them*, to lose yourself. You give those girls at school too much power over you. You could be okay being alone. Solitude is the ultimate sober." He blushes a little when he says this and nervously fingers the thick gold chain he wears over his tight gray T-shirt.

Cyndi smiles a little manically. She seems hyped from all the attention.

"Wow, Ali. I totally hear that," she says. Everyone nods, even little Maria.

"Great feedback, Ali. Direct, concrete, observant," James says in his crisp, in-charge-of-the-universe voice.

I feel the need to contribute, suddenly, not because I have anything specific to say to Cyndi, but because I need to hear my own voice. "Can I add on?" I ask. The words come out high-pitched, uncertain. Everyone turns to stare. I'm making a fatal mistake. I can already tell.

"Maybe," I start, "the girls at school act that way because you have them in a kind of box. It's like you're not seeing them for who they really are, so they can't see you for who you are. I think you may come off defensive and angry toward them."

As soon as the words leave my lips I know it's all wrong. James nods, but his eyes dim. Cyndi turns away. Ali shakes his head. Martin stares, looking hostile.

Ali speaks first. In a low, serious tone he says, "Marcelle, you're really shitting on Cyndi." James cocks his head thoughtfully and strokes his chin. Cyndi turns her cold, chiseled face to me. Maria sits bolt upright, almost bouncing in her seat. I'm afraid I've made enemies of both Martin and Cyndi for good.

I'm reminded of my first day at the Center. "Do you know what a human being is?" Kevin asked me at intake. I figured I should know the answer to such a basic question, but I was so exhausted I just shook my head. "No, Marcelle?" he asked, his white teeth flashing from someplace deep within his beard. "That's the first true thing you've said since you walked in this door, kid. No. You don't know. You know why?" I shook my head again. "Because you're a user and users can't know. You want to be a god. Like all users. I was Kevin the God. But you know what I am now? A man. Someone who knows what it is to mess up and admit it. Someone who has humility, and who can accept both pleasure and pain. You, Marcelle, do not have humility. You want your life to be a free ride, filled with nothing but praise and love. That's for gods, kid, not human beings."

I was confused, and a part of me wanted to give in to nervous laughter, but something in Kevin's look kept me from making a sound. The entire interview was terrifying. It was like Kevin could read my mind, but then twisted everything he found there.

I stare at the ceiling, take a deep breath, and choke back my tears. I can't apologize to Cyndi. The only way forward is through the pile of shit I just dumped on myself. "I don't know," I mutter. "I guess if you're like me you're pissed all the time that you're the one who has to be sober and think about how fucked up your life is, while everyone else gets to go around doing whatever they want."

I'm having a breakdown, and I can't tell how much is real, how much is exhaustion, and how much is me trying to get out of taking abuse for what I said to Cyndi.

I choke on my own snot and Cyndi herself hands me a tissue. "My friends are about a hundred times more fucked up than me. I can't even tell you how bad. But I'm the one here. I'm the one who can't do anything or go anywhere because of one fucking horrible night," I say. I'm crying hard, shoulders shaking. "Everyone around me—my parents, people at school, they're all oblivious to what's really going on." The Group stares. I don't say anything else. I just sit there, crying, finally letting out the sobs I've held in all day long.

"Oblivious?" I hear James ask encouragingly. "Why is everyone you know oblivious?"

Cyndi frowns. Ali drums nervously on the table. Martin rolls his football-player shoulders. Maria stares at her ratty little fingernails. I know peer group is confidential. No one can repeat what they've heard, not even to Kevin. I know they're waiting for more. I get the sense that they are all-in, feeling my fear. For the first time, I feel like a part of the Group. My voice shakes as I try to explain what I know.

"Hannah, Senna, and Chuck are into blow," I say, not delving into the whole complicated mess. It's too soon to tell the whole story—anything that'll get Hannah and everyone else into real trouble. "Hannah's my best friend, okay? And last night she asked me to cover for her—to lie for her—and I did. At the time it didn't seem like that big a deal. Then her mother called my mother, and even then I didn't come clean that Hannah asked me to cover for her. And then she wasn't in school today. I haven't heard anything from her and neither have the guys, her boyfriend, even.

"I'm thinking maybe she ran away to her dad's in New Jersey. I think maybe she's trying to get away from this guy, Alex."

There is silence around the table.

Then James speaks softly. "Marcelle, if your friend is really missing, and she texted you last night, and you concealed this information from her mother, you need to call her mother now. I think you know this." Everyone nods.

"You need to tell your parents what you did," Cyndi adds. I start crying again. "Secret-keeping for your friend isn't going to protect her."

"I know," I say. "I fucked up." My voice sounds small and hoarse.

As we all file out of the Group room, Martin lightly pats my back. I begin to wonder if he and Cyndi really are a thing, or if Martin is just a touchy kind of guy. Cyndi doesn't say a word to anyone as she gets her bag and struts toward the door, her six-month book balanced on the top of her head.

Everyone leaves but me and James. "Later y'all," Maria calls in her singsongy child's voice. "Good luck, Marcelle!" She grins, flashing rows of tiny teeth. For the first time it occurs to me that Maria might be so small not because of her eating disorder, but because she's actually a child—maybe only twelve or thirteen. I wave back wordlessly as James and I slip into Kevin's office.

"This is a good opportunity for you, actually," James says brightly. He sits in Kevin's big faux leather office chair, which makes him look smaller, and paler.

"Now you can walk the walk," he says. "When people first get here, it's mostly all talk and that's great, but it can backfire, too. You get too confident, but you've really done nothing to change yourself. Real work needs action, and you're really lucky to get to take an action in your first month here."

I tap my fingers on Kevin's desk and nod as if I agree with everything James says. In reality, I wish I could be anywhere but Kevin's claustrophobic office. I blink back my tears. No one cares about tears at the Center. No one wants to know how sorry you are.

I text Mom asking for her to come inside to Kevin's office. James looks down at his phone and doesn't look up until Mom comes in.

TEN

I CAN TELL Mom's looking around for an adult, but there aren't any here. Somewhere, there's a janitor named Sam, who pushes around a musty-smelling mop every evening at six, and there's a security guard on the first floor by the elevator, but inside the Center's meeting rooms, there's often just kids at this time of day. Kevin's assistant, Jen, and the other counselors come and go on their own schedule. If any of them are around, they're in their cubicles in the outer offices doing paperwork. James keeps his keys to the metal doors around his neck on a blue nylon lanyard, a sign of his official role.

Mom looks quizzically at James. I try to see James through her eyes. He's really just an awkward kid with too-bright blue eyes, bad skin, and a prominent Adam's apple. His hands, I notice, are very white, and his fingers are long and thin. As he reaches out to shake my mother's hand, I catch a glimpse of the purplish, healed-over track mark on the exposed white of his wrist. I hope Mom doesn't see it too. At the Center, we don't judge where people have been. It's one of the fundamental rules. It's right on the back cover of the handbook: *Here, you are free. You live in the present moment. We offer you the critical support you need to remain free from the suffering of addiction.*

This is not how Mom's mind works. She's told me since I was a little kid: you have to make good choices, so you don't have any regrets. I've always thought of regrets like clouds that line your mind. Regrets are like weather, always there. Even on a clear day, there's something on the horizon, some smudge of gray.

James looks Mom directly in the eye in a way I've come to think of as the Center Look. She seems impressed with him, blind to the scarred wrist.

"Thanks so much for coming in, Marcelle's Mom," James says. "I'm James, Marcelle's group leader. I'm here to support Marcelle and yourself in this conversation, which Marcelle thinks might be a difficult one. I will be mostly a witness, unless there's some reason for me to intervene." I get the feeling "support" in this case also means "eavesdrop on."

James continues, "Marcelle's Mom, I'm not sure you know about our basic principles of communication, so I'll go over the Three Rules. One is we say what we mean and own it. That basically means we choose our words carefully and do not deny our own truth. The second is we listen actively to the other person without rushing to judgment. We respect that the person probably knows right from wrong, and we can help her catch her own accountability. The third is we do our best to understand things as they are, without making things seem better or worse than the reality—we honor the path we're on. Okay?" James rushes through these ground rules, as if it's all common sense, stuff everyone talks about, and not a paragraph from the Center manual that he's been trained to repeat in meetings like this one. Mom turns her gaze to me, drops her nice-to-meet-you smile, and crosses her arms.

She's tired of waiting.

"What now?" she asks, looking at me sharply. "Tell me right now, Marcelle. I have no time for this." She nods in James's direction as though suddenly she sees him as my protector. James sinks into Kevin's chair, expressionless, nodding to go on.

I wipe the tears from my face and sit up straight. "At first, it didn't seem like a big deal," I say. "It just seemed like Hannah didn't want Senna to know where she was going. I thought maybe she was seeing another guy, so I didn't tell you that she asked me to lie for her last night." I pause and try to think what happened next. "But she didn't answer any of my texts all night, and then she didn't come to school today and everyone else was there," I continue. "She's still not answering her phone. No one else knows where she is either, not Senna or Chuck." I exhale loudly. I feel my chest and throat tighten.

At first, Mom looks relieved. She's obviously glad this is not a story about me getting supplied with vodka or beer by one of my friends. Then she seems to give the story some thought. She takes off her glasses, and her face is blankly angry.

I glance at James and he nods, calmly urging me on. He even reaches out and puts his hand on my shoulder. I want to say it's not my fault—that I don't control Hannah—no one does.

"I'm sorry," I say. "I should have told you right away, and I should have told Elise when she called." James gives me a squeeze. I think I must weigh twenty pounds more than him, and that my shoulder must feel big to the touch, but he leaves his hand there. I am, in some non-physical way, smaller than James. I'm small on the inside.

Mom breathes deeply, and to my surprise, she tears up.

"All I know," Mom finally says, "is this has gone too far. If Hannah has run away, and her mother and the police can't find her, you are in part responsible. Do you understand that?" Her hands clench into bony fists. "Marcelle, it seems like you are constantly looking for a way to avoid meeting our most basic expectations."

Mom looks from James back to me, back to James again. "This is not a healthy relationship between my daughter and Hannah Scott." She shakes her head and sighs. "She lets Hannah walk all over her. I honestly think it's how Marcelle got into *this* situation in the first place."

She looks back at me and continues, "You have to have your own values—your own ideas about what's right and what's wrong. You need to stand up for yourself. Tell Hannah you will *not* keep covering for her!"

I look to James, who slowly raises his eyebrows. Then he cocks his head and holds his hand to his ear, miming what I have to do. Mom holds out her cell phone. "Do the right thing, Marcelle," she says.

I take my Mom's phone, find Elise's number on the recent calls list, and dial.

There's a pause when I tell Elise about Hannah's text. For a millisecond I expect her to say Hannah is home in bed, that she's been home for hours.

"Marcelle," Elise says finally. "What did you say?"

I start to repeat myself, but Elise Scott interrupts, and I hand my Mom the phone. Elise must be going nuts, because my mom is mostly listening, except for saying things like she understands and she would feel the same way. Then Mom nods and says, "Yes, Elise, I would."

"She's letting the police know," Mom says. "She's been speaking to them since last night, but this information could help. They've told Elise that with runaways, it's difficult. They can't send out a huge search party for someone who doesn't want to be found. The fact she texted you makes it seem as though she had a definite plan, which I suppose is the good news, in a way. At least she didn't just run off without thinking."

I glance at James, but he's staring out the window at some kids waiting for the bus. He looks bored, as if this sort of drama goes on at the Center all the time. Maybe in James's experience these things turn out all right; missing girls show up, scars heal, track marks get concealed, and life goes on—fucked up, but continuous. Maybe the Center feels inevitable to James, like varsity sports, graduation, and college for other people.

Mom and I walk to her car in silence. Once again, she's favoring her right leg, holding her knee in a stiff, awkward position. Climbing into the spotless beige interior of her Acura, I feel a little less like a criminal than I did in Kevin's office. I did what I needed to do. I told Elise Scott what I know, or at least everything that seems immediately relevant.

Mom looks straight ahead as she drives. If things had gone normally for me this year, I'd be driving right now. I'd have my permit and I'd be practicing for my road test. But Mom and Dad agreed that would all have to wait until my six months at the Center are up.

Dad left my mangled, blood-and-mud-splattered Hampton Classic by the curb on the Friday after my Death Wish crash, the day you leave out the really big stuff you want to get rid of. I think he did it to show me he didn't care who knew what happened, that we were beyond that. One wheel of the bike was bent almost in half. The handlebars were twisted, with one pointing practically straight up. It looked dead, if you can say that about an inanimate object.

At the light at Myrtle, Mom brakes too suddenly, and I jolt forward. She shoots me a look. "Sorry," she says. "I'm distracted—just thinking about Elise. I don't know how she's coping." Mom shakes her head. "It's unreal to me that Hannah would do this to her mother. What could she possibly be thinking?" The light turns, and Mom sighs, rubbing her knee as she accelerates up the hill. "I don't think I need to tell you how disappointed I am that you lied like this, Marcelle, even if you thought you were protecting a friend. It's just wrong."

"I know, Mom," I say. "I get that. I didn't know what else to do. I'm really sorry. I want you guys to trust me."

When Mom seems to accept what I've said, I go on. "Anyway, why don't parents realize kids just fuck themselves up? Why do they have to make things worse by taking everything so personally?"

Mom turns and frowns at me. "Marcelle, this isn't the time for your philosophies on life. You really aren't looking that smart at the moment."

I stare out the window and let the warm tears roll down my cheeks. "I don't think being a fuck-up means I can't be smart, too," I mumble. But Mom doesn't respond. She just keeps driving.

ELEVEN

BACK IN THE neighborhood, Mom parks at the curb in front of Michiko's house.

We sit in silence for what feels like an eternity. "I know it's hard," Mom finally says, and I nod, even though she's being vague, and I'm still angry in a way I can't explain.

I pause with my hand on the car door, and peer at the place in the trees that opens onto the Death Wish path. There is a short, steep, rock-filled drop from the trail onto the road opposite Michiko's driveway. I don't know how many times I've taken that path across town. Hundreds, probably.

"Don't take long," Mom says, putting the car back into drive.

"I won't," I say. "But remember, I'm walking home." I don't mean to remind her about my wrecked bike, but I don't need her texting me every other minute asking why I'm not home yet. I'm still slightly amazed she's leaving me at Michiko's on my own. I expected, once I confessed about Hannah, I would be on immediate, total lockdown, but after her brief flare-up, Mom seems to be back to thinking the drama with Hannah is mainly Elise's problem, not hers. I want to think this too—that Hannah is going to show up and my life will return to semi-normal.

I get the mail out of the plain, silver mailbox and unlock the front door of Michiko's house.

After the accident, my parents asked Michiko if there was a way I could compensate her for the hassle of having a drunk girl nearly die in front of her house at three in the morning. She hadn't hesitated. "I get home and the bird is squawking, and the cat is underfoot, begging for his dinner, and all I want to do is sit down with a glass of wine. I've been thinking for a long time how I need a housekeeper, but just for fifteen minutes a day!"

Michiko laughed when she said this, and I think my parents found it strange, given the fact they saw my "job" as a form of punishment. The three of us had walked over to Michiko's the Sunday evening after the accident to apologize and offer up my services. I was annoyed with my parents for coming with me, when I'd already promised to go on my own.

There was a dinner plate–size bloodstain visible on the grayish asphalt driveway that Dad casually sidestepped. Mom rang the doorbell, and I remember feeling like I was about to vomit just being there. When Michiko answered the door, she was wearing what looked like white pajama bottoms with a white sweater, even though it was only four or five in the afternoon. She was barefoot, and I remember finding it strange that she was dressed identically to how I remember seeing her the night of the crash, standing there in the dark with her cat, the two of them all I could make out before the darkness around them narrowed, then caved in on me.

I walk around the house, switching on every light as I go. I call out to Marco and on cue he darts around the corner and pounces on my feet as I turn into the kitchen. He bats my ankles, but he keeps his claws harmlessly retracted. This is his usual semi-aggressive greeting.

It smells mysteriously good everywhere at Michiko's, like a spa, but it's also dark, and a little frightening. When I get Marco his food, and his attention is turned safely to his bowl, I turn on the outside lights and the lights over the kitchen table, and text Andy.

At Michiko's is all I say. Then I put the phone in the pocket of my overalls and begin the rest of my chores. I switch on all the lights in the four rooms on the main floor of the house.

Michiko's husband is gone, wherever asshole husbands go. That's what she told me, anyway.

The tuna smell is strong and makes me want to gag, but Marco sticks his whole face in the bowl and eats. I'm about to text Andy a second time, when my phone vibrates in my pocket.

"Hello?" I say. My heart skips a beat.

"Hey, Marci, what's going on?" he asks. I exhale slowly and begin my story. I start about Hannah's mom, and how I had to call her from the Center in front of Mom and James. It feels like forever ago now, and telling the story exhausts me.

There's a long silence. "Where do you think she went?" I

picture Andy, his dark eyes, his smallish mouth, the square white teeth that are his best feature.

"I don't know," I say. "But her mom is going nuts. You're probably going to get a call."

For a moment, I imagine Hannah, her tiny body, the brass bracelet she always wears pushed up onto her bicep. I picture Senna, the bear, his narrow green eyes, his thick torso. Hannah made more sense with Chuck—delicate, beautiful Chuck. But none of that matters now, their love triangle, Hannah's playing on Senna's jealousy. Senna and Chuck were both in school today. Hannah went wherever Hannah went alone, or at least not with either of them.

After a long pause Andy says, "Maybe they'll all get the crap scared out of them—and Jonas will go to a real college, and Hannah and Senna will see that Alex is a loser drug-dealer asshole." It's like Andy has read my mind.

"Yeah, that would be a dream come true," I say. "If they could forget they ever met that scum. Senna seemed pretty pissed this morning, about the knife or whatever last night. So maybe."

It's true I could see Senna turning on Alex. He could be jealous, or hold a grudge about Alex threatening him, but could Hannah, I wonder? Hannah crossed a line. She crossed it with Alex. He knew he could get her to do whatever he wanted. There are people like that, people who can read you, and don't care how they use what they know. Somehow, I think she respected him for that—for seeing her craziness—that part of her that doesn't care about anything but the moment she's in, the high she's chasing. "I think it might be too late," I say. "She's already gone too far."

There's a heavy silence. "Don't say that," Andy says. "Don't panic. I think we should hold on—don't say too much, yet. If we do, everyone's screwed."

"Yeah," I say. "I guess you're right."

"I can't sell out my own brother. Not like this. Not this fast."

"I know," I say.

"If we tell about what Alex and Jonas are doing, and she comes back, then what? Everyone will know what she did. How could she come back to school? It'll be a huge fucking deal. Jesus, I don't know. I don't want them all to get arrested. I don't want to have to talk to the cops. I want them to stop on their own."

"I know," I say, my heart racing. I agree with Andy, but I'm also scared about tomorrow—what happens if she's still not back? But Andy keeps talking. Like me, he's confused—scared and confused. I want him to know more—to be sure about something, but how could he be?

"Unless, you think . . . I don't know. I don't want to tell you what to do. Or not do." Andy trails off. "I mean, I understand if you feel like you have to. Either way, I'm not going to say anything to Senna or anyone, if you tell. I just can't do it. Not yet."

Of course, that's the question. Neither of us wants to rat, if we can help it. But what if Hannah is in some kind of trouble? What if she hasn't run away, and what she was doing with Alex is a clue to finding her?

"I don't know what to think," I say. "She must have had some reason to want to run. Like if something went on with Alex. Something she couldn't control." I think about what she said about the men who watched her. They could be anyone. Could some guy, some stranger, have tracked her down?

My throat feels dry and my eyes burn. "I'm just going to hope she shows up tomorrow," I say. "I promised I'd never tell anyone. I can't break that promise because of one day. One night. Never is supposed to be never."

"That's what I think," Andy says. "Well, not about never, but about for now. Call me if anything happens."

"I can't. I'm blacked out. I'm supposed to turn my phone off when I get home," I say. "So, good night, I guess."

"Good night," he says. "Take care of yourself, Marci. Shit has rained down on you long enough. You don't need this. You're, like, the only one of us with nothing to do with Alex."

I smile to myself. I'm not sure Andy realizes no one else in my life calls me Marci, but I like that he does. "Yeah. I know. Hannah has no right to go missing when I'm supposed to be the fuck-up of the group."

"It's kind of true," Andy says. There's a long pause, and then he says my name again, I suppose to fill the silence.

"Yeah?" I say.

"I'm sorry I've been kind of distant," he says. "I wanted things to get better, not worse."

"I know," I say.

"I want to see you," he says. "Now that things really are better. I mean, for you. Or sort of better, not counting today."

"Me too," I say. "I'll see you tomorrow in Writing." I know this isn't what he means, but I'm too tired to think what to say.

"Okay," he says quietly. "I'll see you tomorrow. Remember, think positive."

I exhale slowly. "You too." I feel an ache deep in my chest as I hang up. *Think positive*, I tell myself. But what does that really mean?

I can't be sure of anything.

TWELVE

WHEN I LET myself in through the kitchen door, there is an eerie absence of cooking sounds, and no chatter of Mom's news radio.

I find Dad on the couch in the living room. He's wearing his work clothes—button-down shirt and neatly pressed khakis—what he normally wears under his lab coat. He has on the small, round glasses that make his face look too big. His wavy gray-and-black hair is mussed, as though he's been raking it with his hands. Mom sits across from Dad, looking tired and pale.

The real surprise, though, is that they are not alone. My heart drops into my stomach when I see Elise Scott perched on the stiff brown leather chair no one in our family ever sits in. Her hair is combed back smooth, her hands folded on her lap. Her fingernails are short and speckled with dark paint. She looks up as I enter the room, but she doesn't say anything to acknowledge me.

"Sit down, Marcelle," Dad says.

I sit on the edge of the yellow sofa, next to Mom. Elise takes a sip of water, then licks her lips. Dad looks at the floor, or some spot on his brown loafers. "Elise has something to tell you," Mom says.

Elise stares at me, starts to speak, stops and runs her fingers through her cropped hair, then begins once more. "After you called, I talked to the police again. They have an all-county alert posted, but they need more information. She used you to lie, Marcelle. You need to tell us *everything* you know. The police can't be effective without more information. They need to know if Hannah has run away, or if maybe this is something else. . . ." She trails off; her voice quivers.

"Elise did us the favor of coming here herself," Dad says ominously. If I get his drift, he means I could be at the police station, talking to a cop instead.

Elise's eyes are wide and her full mouth is set in a very Hannah-like expression. Hannah is a hard person to say no to and I'm discovering Elise is the same. I squirm.

I think about Alex, Jonas, and Senna. I can almost hear my own heartbeat. If I tell my parents and Elise everything, and I spill about the coke dealing and Hannah doing stuff for Alex's webcam business, all of my friends will be in real trouble. Not just my friends. Andy's brother, too. My head spins. I can't focus on any one line of thinking. My tongue feels thick in my mouth. Andy and I just agreed we'd wait it out. We agreed that it would be best for Hannah—if Hannah comes back—if no one has snitched.

"Marcelle, please start from the beginning. Tell us, and Hannah's mom, whatever you know right now. Elise has had an awful twenty-four hours, and some of that is on you, sweetheart." Dad speaks calmly, but I can tell he's furious at me for lying. He leans toward me, urging me on, and I try to think where to start.

I clear my throat, and Mom hands me a tissue from the box she holds in her lap. I start talking, not knowing where I'll end up. "She texted me around seven. She asked me to cover for her. To tell you she was with me and to say the same thing to Senna. That's it."

"And did you lie to Robert Senna?" Elise asks. "What did he say?"

"No, I didn't. He didn't ask. I only lied to you when I said she was going over there. I never talked to her, and she never said that. She just texted and said 'cover for me.' That's all."

Elise stares at me and then at my parents. "Was she avoiding Robert?" Elise asks. I shrug. It seemed this way to me at the time, but I don't want to go down that road. I don't tell them anything about Alex. I don't tell them about Senna going to Alex's, or about Alex and the knife, or his roommate with the baseball bat.

"This is confusing, Marcelle," Dad says. "Why did she tell you to tell her mother and Robert that she was with you? What was she doing, and who was she with?"

"I don't know," I say. "That's what I asked her, but then she didn't answer. Actually, my text was undelivered. I tried texting her and calling her a lot. But she didn't answer."

Elise sighs and puts her head in her hands. When she does this, she looks even more like Hannah, crouched and small. Then, as though it takes her superhuman strength, Elise sits up straight and exhales. "Someone found her phone, Marcelle," she says. "I'm not able to say where, but it was found by a local dog walker. It was in a strange location. A place . . . a place the police don't think she would go. Not alone. A park ranger had turned it in, and no one thought anything of it until I reported Hannah missing. What you're saying makes it sound like she's run away. If she's running, we need to think of where she'd go. If something else is going on, the police must have that information. What you tell us matters. You are the last person she communicated with before she lost that phone."

I freeze.

"What about her dad?" I ask. "Did you get ahold of him? Could she be with him?"

Elise shakes her head. "He isn't answering either. He could be out of the country. I can't keep track of his schedule. *He* can't keep track of his schedule. He could be in the Amazon, for all I know." My mind races. I can't process what Elise Scott is saying. I think of the places the dog walkers go in town—there's the Death Wish, but there's other places, too. But nothing makes sense. If she ran away, Hannah would *need* her phone.

"He has no secretary you can call? A company he works with over there?" Dad asks.

Elise shakes her head. "He hasn't got two nickels to rub together. He runs his whatever he calls it—chocolate-consulting business—out of that crap apartment in Jersey City."

"So she *could* be at his place?" I say. My heart lightens at this thought. It's possible Hannah's father is away, and she wants absolutely no one to know where she is. This makes perfect sense, and I almost laugh aloud at the thought. Hannah needs to get sober, to chill out, and maybe this is the only way she could think of to get some rest.

I can connect the dots in my head, but I can hardly explain my thoughts to the adults, who continue to stare at me blankly. Then I remember Hannah's missed audition, and all the hope I felt only a moment ago vanishes. Hannah wouldn't miss her audition just for a few days' rest.

"I've given the police his address," Elise says. "And they're in communication with the New Jersey authorities."

I nod.

"Marcelle, you are not to share this information with any-one, do you understand?"

I hear the voice, but I feel small and far away, as if I were at the bottom of an empty pool. The police are investigating. What does this mean? I can't think straight.

"Maybe she doesn't want to be tracked?" I say. "Maybe she got one of those cheap phones and she'll call?" I'm rambling.

"Okay, Marcelle," Dad says, taking his glasses off and rubbing them with the corner of his shirt. "Why don't you go eat the dinner left in the kitchen, do whatever homework you have, and get some sleep."

"Okay," I murmur. I lean over and give Elise Scott a light

hug. She catches my hand. Her grasp is surprisingly strong.

"She missed the audition," she says, shaking her head. "I wouldn't think she'd miss that for the world. I kept expecting her to walk in the door with some crazy explanation for staying out all night. Right up until four o'clock, I was sure she'd come. I even thought about calling the music school to see if she'd shown up on her own."

I stare at Elise, but what I see in my mind is Hannah's face. I'm not psychic. I don't believe any of that. But in my mind I can picture Hannah, very pale and very thin. I can see her white hands locked together, her hair, as always, in a pretty tangle across her face.

I start to cry, and no one jumps to comfort me. I walk out of the room, my face in my hands. I'm shaking. I don't eat like Dad told me to. I need to get upstairs; I need to think.

I'm afraid of what I know and haven't said, but I'm also afraid to say anything more. If I rat on Hannah and Senna, and tell about Alex, they'll all be in trouble—even Hannah could be arrested when she comes back, if she comes back. I need to talk to Andy. Dad said I can't tell anyone about Hannah's phone. They said it was a police matter, like there is some legal reason I'm not supposed to talk. But I need to tell someone, and Andy is the one person I know I can trust. Tomorrow. We can talk tomorrow.

THIRTEEN

WHEN MOM PULLS into the line of traffic in front of school, I glance toward the small hill next to the football field to see if the guys are waiting under the tree. I see Chuck's lone thin figure. "Marcelle," Mom says as she puts the car in park, "keep your head on straight, okay? I know this is hard. We're all really worried about Hannah." She rubs her bad leg, and purses her lips in obvious pain. In the bright sunlight, I can see all the gray hairs standing out from the dark ones on her head, and all the wrinkles near her eyes and across her forehead. I think, randomly, that fear makes everyone look the same—everyone gets the same grayness, the same shadows under their eyes.

"I know," I say. My stomach growls noisily. I was late getting up and had neither coffee nor food this morning, and no dinner last night. I know I should get out of the car, but I can't make myself move.

Mom sighs. "It's not your fault Hannah has made the choices she's made, and we're glad you told the truth yesterday about her texts to you on Sunday night. But having good judgment means making the right choices in the moment, not after. It's really important you get that—that you really get that now, okay?"

I hum a little, which isn't voluntary, and then I nod, so she knows I'm listening, and I get what she's saying—what she's *been* saying since yesterday at the Center. Cars have begun to line up behind us, and I glance nervously at the stream of kids walking past our car. That's when I catch sight of Andy. He's standing on the sidewalk with his hoodie pulled up. He catches my eye and gives me a small, uncertain smile.

"I'm trying, Mom," I say. "I have to go now. They'll mark me late." I put my hand on the car door and hesitate. I'm not sure what more to say. I know she expects me to tell her I will never lie to her again, or that I know it was wrong to keep Hannah's secrets. But I'm still keeping Hannah's secrets, and I don't know if I can stop. Mom nods sharply. "I know you're trying, Marcelle. Dad and I just want you to try harder. We want you to *think* about what you're doing."

I get out and stand on the sidewalk in my baggy overalls and Doc Martens with my flannel tied around my waist. I don't know whether to laugh or cry. I watch the Acura turn onto Post Road, and a part of me wants Mom to turn back and get me, even if she's angry. I could say that I'm sick, and everyone would finally leave me in peace. It wouldn't be a lie. I feel chilled and slightly nauseous.

I turn to where I saw Andy, but he's moved through the crowd and is now at my side. "Good news," he says brightly.

I feel my heart jump out of my chest. I want to hug him

right there in front of Ms. Harris, the principal, and all the kids streaming through the glass doors. "No, no, Marci," he says. "I'm sorry, not that good. I just mean Bartow is absent. There's a sign on her door. We have first period free."

Normally, I'd be ecstatic to have first period canceled. But Andy knew what I was thinking—that Hannah was there, at school, and that she had come home after all and was no longer missing.

"Shit," I say. "That really got my hopes up, Andy."

"Come on," he says. "I'll buy you a coffee."

Andy and I cross the faculty parking lot, packed with Subarus and Hondas, toward the Starbucks a block and a half away. Inside, there is hardly a line. No one who regularly has first period free bothers to come to school this early. There are a few other kids from Bartow's class, but neither Andy nor I acknowledge them.

In line next to Andy, I feel slightly dizzy. There is too much going on, and too much to say. I realize, suddenly, that I am shaky with hunger, and how lucky I am that Bartow didn't show up for class. Andy asks me what I want, and I say a latte and a bagel. Then I take a ten out of my pocket, but he pushes my hand away. Our fingers briefly touch, and I feel a tingling sensation run through me.

I follow Andy to a table by the window, and when I'm sure no one is listening I explain how Elise was at my house when I got home from Michiko's, and how the cops have found Hannah's phone.

"Her mom is freaking out. It's possible she's at her dad's. But

81

I don't know what the fuck to think." I'm half whispering even though the next closest table is filled with some freshman girls sipping hot chocolate, kids who would have no idea who Hannah Scott even is.

Andy looks serious. "I didn't see Senna this morning," he says. Then he adds, "You had to tell about her text, Marci. No doubt." He reaches across the table for my hand. His eyes are dark and solemn. He blinks his thick lashes rapidly. He gets up and brings me a handful of napkins. I'm crying now, not hard, but enough so that when I dab around my eyes, my makeup smudges.

"I think you should lay low," Andy says. "Try to stay away from Senna. It's not your fault if the cops call him in, but he might blame you. I mean, if she seemed to be avoiding him, they're obviously going to ask him questions."

Technically, it's possible for me to get through the day without seeing Senna. I can avoid the cafeteria, and the halls are so crowded between classes it's easy to act like you don't see someone.

I spread cream cheese on my bagel for something to do with my hands, but I suddenly don't feel like eating. I take a sip of coffee. It's good and hot. Andy leans across the table. "What's it like there, at the Center?" he asks suddenly.

I shrug. I know Andy still feels guilty about my crash. But it isn't his fault. I was falling all summer. That night he said what he had to say—that he wasn't going to be a part of it. I want to tell him how it felt when I fell, but I don't want him to think there's something really wrong with me. I don't want him to think I was trying to hurt myself because of *him*.

I glance at my watch. It's already eight thirty and my next class is across the building, a ten-minute walk. I hesitate. "Do you remember that night of my crash?" I ask Andy.

Andy nods and leans back in his chair. "I remember," he says. "I'm sorry, Marci. I shouldn't have let you leave like that. I was trying to talk to you for weeks. But you kept running away from me. That one time I walked you home, and we were both fucked up, was when I realized—I don't want it to be like that. That's how Jonas is. He's always giving girls blow and trying to fuck them. He talks about how much *pussy* he and Alex get because of it. Because of the coke. I can't listen to them. It's just not who I am. I want you to know I think you're a great girl, and that's all. I never meant it to seem any other way. I always liked you."

I'm crying more now, and I don't really care about my makeup. "I'm sorry," I say, although I'm not sure what I'm apologizing for. Then I tell him about what I remember from the Death Wish night. I tell him about my ride through the woods, how fast I was going, and how I kind of let go. "I don't think I was trying to get hurt," I say. "But it's like I stopped trying to stay on my bike. I wasn't scared when I fell, not like I should have been."

Andy nods. "Everyone was fucked up. I knew I should have done something when you left. I knew you were upset. But I just wanted to get home. I just wanted to get the fuck out. Not to get away from you, but *them*. The whole scene over there at Senna's." He paused, dropped his head into his hands, and looked up. He had tears in his eyes. "Jonas doing that shit with Alex makes me sick. I think my parents know something is up, too, because Jonas is never home, and when he is he seems pretty high. Anyway, if they find out about the girls—even if Jonas just does the tech stuff for Alex, my parents will literally die. Or they'll kill him." He took a breath, drank some coffee, and went on. "My dad is a freaking engineer. He keeps asking Jonas about the app, and Jonas tells him it's a game in real time, but nothing else."

We stare at each other for a minute without speaking; I guess because we're too scared to say anything more. I reach for my book bag. "I have to get to class," I say softly. I wrap my bagel in my napkin, and stand up. "I knew since September," I say. "Hannah told me what they were doing and I didn't try to stop her."

Andy scoffs. "There isn't any way of stopping any of them. Unless maybe Hannah found one."

"What do you mean?" I ask.

"I really don't know," Andy says. "But if she did run away, maybe she knew what she was doing."

Andy stands, grabs his own book bag, and leads us toward the exit.

When we get outside he turns to me. "Are you going to be at Michiko's again tonight?" he asks.

"Yeah," I say. "Around six."

"I can meet you there?" he says. He tilts his head and half smiles. I feel myself blush. "But I don't want to get you in trouble," he adds. "We could hang out. I could help you with whatever you're doing."

"Okay," I say. "I'll ride my old street bike over. No one will know. Michiko never gets home before eight."

We head in silence toward the main building. Andy walks close to me, but we never actually touch. Then Andy puts his arm around me and gives me a half hug. My face burns. I turn toward the A building and the glass-enclosed hallway of the language classrooms, then glance back, catch Andy's eye, and wave. Time seems slowed down. My heart feels strangely light, but I can feel a darkness creep over me as I walk away. I still have the entire day to get through, and know nothing more about Hannah.

There's a dog park up past Senna's house, near the elementary school. Sometimes, Hannah likes to walk there. But there's the beach, too, a place down by the Sound, filled with cattails and long, wild grasses. There are the trails near the public pool in White Plains, where I once went swimming with my dad and my uncle. There are woods all around our town. In almost every neighborhood, there's some trail that leads somewhere else; back behind the houses, between the streets, there are trees and little streams, and giant moss-covered boulders, and tall, tall grasses. Her phone must have been in one of these out-of-the-way places, someplace Elise called *strange*.

What the fuck, Hannah? I think. *Where the fuck are you?*

FOURTEEN

" **LOOK WHO'S GOING** our way, Chuck. My faithful friend Marcelle." Senna and Chuck suddenly appear on either side of me as I pass through the heavy metal doors out of the main building on my way across the leaf-strewn courtyard to French.

The three of us walk in an uncomfortable silence in the general direction of the C building, until Senna suddenly slows, leans toward me, and hisses, "Now'd be the time, Marcelle."

I tug on the end of my braid. I can feel my throat constrict. Like everyone else, Senna thinks I know more than I do. I decide the best tactic, the most effective way to get him off my back, is to tell him what I *do* know.

"Hannah's mom came over last night," I begin, and then I start doing the fast-talking thing I do whenever I'm really nervous. "I got the third degree from her and my parents. There was one text from Hannah, that's all, on Sunday. The cops told

Elise Scott there's not enough evidence for a full-on search. They say it looks too much like Hannah ran away. They don't do search parties for runaways—there are too many places to go, too many fucked-up kids out there. They're telling Elise to contact everyone Hannah knows, including people she's in contact with on social media." I shoot Senna a look. My head hurts. I need to get to French. I'm blabbering. I'm not really even sure how much of what I'm saying is true. I can't actually remember what Elise Scott said about the cops. Then I remember about her dad's. "It's possible she's hiding out at her dad's for some reason. He's out of the country. I think Elise is checking his place, too." I pause. I wonder how much of what I'm saying Senna already knows.

Chuck looks at his phone, but I feel like he, like Senna, is hanging on my every word. I have to remind myself repeatedly to breathe.

"So what did you say, Marcelle? Did you spill your guts to Mom and Dad? Or to your little rehab buddies? Because now might be the time to tell me. Or do you want all of us busted?" Senna stops and turns toward me. Chuck stops too, still looking at his phone, but leaning in so close our elbows almost touch. "I know she told you about Alex," Senna says. "I told her not to, but she likes to show off." He shakes his head. "I would have thought she'd want to keep that quiet. But she's too fucking crazy to keep her mouth shut about anything."

My throat is so dry I almost can't speak. "I haven't said anything," I say. "Why would I? I'm guessing she'll turn up in a day or two." I'm not making sense, exactly, but this is all I can think to say. Senna looks off into the distance. Kids stream by us in both directions—jocks in game-day jerseys, skinny freshman boys, a tall, long-haired girl from my gym class who nods hello. I'm nervous about being late to French. Ms. Lawrence can be a hard-ass and might give me after-school study hall if I'm late, which I can't attend because of Group.

"I don't know, Marce," Senna says. "This sucks, though. Fucking sucks the bitch can't send one text to let me know where the fuck she went."

I look at Senna, incredulous. The edges of his mouth are pulled downward in a contortion of grief or fear. It's not what I thought. Senna looks scared, hurt, like a guy whose girlfriend took off without a word, and who really just wants her to come back.

If this is an act, it's flawless.

"I know, Rob," I say, using the name I haven't called him in years. "I swear I'll tell you if I hear anything. Okay?" I pat Senna on the shoulder, and he feels stiff. I start to walk away, and when I turn back to look at them, Chuck and Senna are still just standing there, Senna with his thumbs looped in the straps of his book bag, staring at nothing. Chuck is still looking at his phone, but standing close to Senna, like he's about to show him something on his screen.

I make it to the second floor of the C building as the bell rings, and half run down the hallway and around the corner to class just late enough to draw attention to my entrance.

Everyone looks up when I walk in, but I duck and make my way to my seat in the back. Ms. Lawrence shoots me a look, but it's more like concern than annoyance. I give her a small apologetic smile, open my iPad, and start tapping away like I have a clue what I'm supposed to be doing.

My head pounds. I'm so confused, I pull out my math textbook instead of my French book and the girl next to me points at it and laughs. I lean down to switch books but then stop halfway.

The reality of what's happening hits me all at once: the police may not be organizing a search party for Hannah yet, but they are investigating her disappearance. Her text to me on Sunday is a clue. Her phone was found in some isolated place everyone is keeping secret.

Whoever knows where her phone was found could be some sort of suspect. I have no idea what Senna or any of the guys know, and except for the stuff I've told them, including Andy, they don't know what I know.

Whatever else is going on, I am now part of an investigation. I scan the classroom, surprised that no one seems to be looking at me. It's amazing how the world can go on around you, when in your own mind you know nothing can ever be the same.

FIFTEEN

THAT AFTERNOON, I stand in front of the glass doors, sweating. They say it's almost seventy, which seems wrong for this time of year. I'm wearing my flannel to conceal the pit stains on my gray tank.

When I get in the car, Mom hands me a bag with a bunch of apple slices and cubes of cheese in it, like I'm a toddler. I stuff the bag in my backpack without saying thanks, but at least I don't say anything nasty about the baby snacks.

I pull down the sun visor and examine my face in the mirror behind it, looking for visible evidence of my fucked-up state of mind, but I look surprisingly normal. My eyes are clear, since I'm not hungover. My scar is less rough-looking, the pink line beginning to blend with my complexion. I'm looking good, for me. But I stare at my reflection a second too long and catch a glimpse of the fear in my own eyes.

I try to picture her: Hannah at her dad's, curled up on the

leather couch, her jacket and boots on, hair matted to her head, looking disheveled but safe. I realize this is an actual memory from the time we stayed at her dad's after the Brick concert at Man-Ray's in Jersey City. I try to conjure her somewhere else.

But no, nothing.

I shudder. In study hall, Mr. White hadn't said anything about Hannah's absence, but you could tell he was more relaxed than usual. Hannah wasn't there to suck the oxygen out of the room by kicking off her silver flats and walking around the room barefoot, like that singer, Delia somebody, with her tangled hair hanging in front of her face, her bracelet pushed way up on her thin arm—everyone captivated, everyone getting the silent, spontaneous joke.

"Did you hear anything from Elise?" I ask Mom. I think of Elise at our house last night, her wide eyes, her Hannah-like frown. It's odd that they aren't closer, since they're so much alike.

Mom nods. "Elise says there was no activity on Hannah's phone after that text to you, Marcelle. Not one text, no posts, nothing." My heart skips a beat. I'm still, as far as anyone knows, the last person to have had contact with Hannah. "Elise is a wreck. I'm sure Beverly is as well. I think Elise's sister is coming to stay with them tonight." I hadn't thought about Beverly, Hannah's thirteen-year-old sister, or how she might be taking all of this. Hannah has a weird protective side to her when it comes to Bev. Any time we partied at Hannah's she made sure she locked her bedroom door so Beverly wouldn't barge in on

us. It was like Hannah wanted Beverly to be completely innocent—to be her opposite in every way.

We pull into the Center parking lot, and I start to sweat
again. My back and underarms are damp, and my upper lip is
moist. I haven't had time yet today to focus on this place, these
people, on James and Cyndi and Kevin, or who I'm supposed to
be when I come here. I know that I need to be sober, and I know
coming to the Center is something I have to do. But I still wish
I could have another chance at normal. More than anything,
I wish Hannah and I both could go back in time. But I know
it's useless to think this way. I am the girl who crashed on the
Death Wish path. I can't be any other girl.

Looking at the entrance to the Center, I feel dizzy, like the
minute I step out of the car I'll fall, not down to the pavement,
but to some distant place, like the way little kids think they can
dig all the way to China—I feel like I could fall and fall and fall.

"Marcelle." Mom looks at me, her mouth a tense line, her
eyes a piercing blue. She hates that I've brought her to this place.
"If you have any more information, you *have* to tell someone.
You can tell me. You can tell your dad. You can tell Kevin,"
she adds, gesturing toward the low brick building in front of
us. "But you cannot, you absolutely cannot keep any information to yourself. Do you understand?" She fixes me again with
a cold, hard stare. "You might think you're protecting Hannah.
Or someone else. But if you're withholding facts, you could be
endangering Hannah. The police are searching the area where
Hannah's phone was found. Marcelle, she hasn't used her bank

card, either. This is just so upsetting." Mom reaches over and pushes a stray hair from my forehead. "I'm sorry, baby," she says. "This seems really serious now."

I look down at my own hands, and see they are clenched into tight fists.

I could tell about Alex, and the room in his apartment with its blacked-out window—Alex's screens, his cameras and lights. I could talk about the sordid scheme Hannah and Senna had to get more money, and more coke. But if I point the way—say something about Senna or Jonas, even Andy might get into trouble. Andy knew what was happening too. He introduced Senna to Jonas, and was basically how everyone got to Alex in the first place. He knew and didn't tell his parents about Jonas. We're all connected. I can't tell a story about just one person.

I grab my bag. My arms feel heavy and clumsy. "Mom," I say, "I think I need to go inside." My voice is just above a whisper.

I get out of the car, and halfway across the parking lot I turn back. Mom hasn't moved. I wonder if she's on her phone, or if she's just sitting there watching me walk away. A part of me wants to run back, and another part of me wants to run away. But I trudge toward the entrance of the building, almost numb, almost forgetting why I am even here.

SIXTEEN

I KNOCK LIGHTLY on the first door in the row of therapy offices. Kevin shouts for me to come in, and I step in tentatively, without speaking, and sit perched on the edge of the small, red-backed, school-type chair next to his desk.

Kevin is hunched over his iPad, tapping his notes with two chubby fingers. He has bushy dark brown hair that seems tall rather than long. His round belly hangs over his worn leather belt—he's a big guy all around, which is one of the few things I like about him.

"So?" Kevin leans back in his chair, and peers at me from under insane eyebrows. I look down. "Is the Personal Responsibility Plan supposed to be written?" I ask. "Or can I just say it?" Kevin stares at me. "Goes in the journal," he says. I was so preoccupied the night before, I was lucky to get my regular work done, never mind my stuff for the Center. My journal is in my backpack in the cubby down the hall, but it doesn't matter because the PRP isn't in it, because I haven't written it yet. Kevin doesn't miss a beat. He hands me a pen out of the pen holder on his desk. He hands me a yellow pad from a drawer. "You're good to go," he says. "No excuses."

Failure isn't really allowed at the Center, which is what Kevin means when he says "no excuses." You can screw up. But you can't not have a plan, or if you *don't* have a plan, someone here will have one for you, at least until you can go it alone.

Failure means someone has your back. Like everything people say at the Center, this seems like a deliberate mind-fuck: they won't let me fail, but I'll be a burden to everyone whenever I don't do the exact right thing.

"Write your Present Three," Kevin says, pointing at the paper, as if I have no idea what the paper is for. The Present Three are my goals for the week or month, however long it takes to make progress. Then I'm supposed to have a plan for meeting these goals each day. That's what a Personal Responsibility Plan is. That's what Kevin and I are supposed to go over during our meetings, until I get on the next phase of the program.

"I'm sorry," I start to say. "My friend Hannah . . ." I begin. But Kevin stares at my yellow pad, waiting for me to start. "Don't you even want to know what's going on?" My voice breaks. I'm angry suddenly. I have something serious to tell him—*Hannah is missing. Hannah's phone has been found. This means something, but I'm afraid of what.* Kevin shakes his head slowly. This isn't therapy where you say what's on your mind. This is therapy where you do what you're told.

"There is always a distraction," Kevin says. "We all have good reasons to use substances to get through the day. Grandma is sick. My dog died. My boyfriend is a dick. *My friend ran away.*" He uses a funny, whiny voice when he says these things. I can hardly believe what I'm hearing. He *knows* about Hannah, most likely from James, but he's saying it doesn't matter—it shouldn't be a distraction to me that my best friend is missing.

"Maybe that pisses you off?" he asks, eyes wide, ready for my reaction. I nod, holding back tears of fury. None of this is fair. "Maybe you want to drink and have a pity party every time someone you care about gets hurt, or fucks themselves up? That's how you help out your friends—you drink away their pain?" He pauses. He can see that I'm upset, and I think for a second he'll stop this rant, but then he goes on. "You're a liar if you say it helps. You know it, too. You're a smart one, Marcellena."

"I didn't *do* anything!" I say. "My best friend is missing and I didn't *do* anything." I'm crying for real now. "Everyone is waiting for me to spill my guts, but I can't! I can't help. And no, I didn't get drunk."

After a few seconds, Kevin smiles.

"I'm sorry about your friend, Marcelle. I really am. But addicts are liars and cheats. Addicts are cowards. Your addict friends will break your heart, not once, but as many times as you let them. Right now, you are one of them. You are an addict. You are breaking people's hearts and scaring the shit out of people, just like your missing friend. An addict can't care.

Your brain is wired wrong. Your brain is about shit and get-ting over. Somewhere in there you have a good mind. But your addict brain has hijacked it. You're starting to fight back, I can see that. But your addict mind is going to try every trick in the book to get back into the driver's seat. Self-pity is a pretty good trick. Works more often than it fails. They can call it 'self-medicating.' But that's bullshit. Total, fucking self-delusional crap. Medicine is for cancer. Or gonorrhea. Or the bloody runs. Maybe, for some, in the case of major depression. But your teen-aged insecurities don't need medicine."

Kevin leans toward me, and I can smell his rancid cof-fee breath. I want to spit in his face, and tell him he doesn't know anything about me, but I just sit there, crying and feeling weirdly detached. I'm angry and scared, but also sort of frozen.

Hannah is somewhere out there. She is an addict, a heart-breaker. But she's also alone, I think, and maybe hurt, or maybe with someone even worse than Alex.

It isn't true, I want to say to Kevin, that you can't love an addict, that you can't save a friend. It isn't true that you can change your life by walking through the doors of some lame brick building in the middle of town. But I can't speak. And anyway, according to Kevin, I'm not a real person yet. I still have an addict brain. I am a subhuman, an unreasonable beast, a worthless sort of being incapable of human connection. If that's true of us all, how does any addict get better?

"Now, stop your crying and write a plan, Marcelle." Kevin interrupts my train of thought. "You won't have any real friends until you're sober at least a month. You probably haven't had a real friend in years. Maybe you don't know how to be a friend, or make a friend. That's true of lots of kids your age. You'd be surprised. So many different kinds of users, using the drugs, using the sex, using the money, you name it. But we'll find out. We'll pop the trunk, drain the lubricants, and take that engine apart piece by piece. We'll see what's working and what's not, my friend."

I begin to write the words *Personal Responsibility Plan* across the top of the yellow pad. I'm still crying, so I can't see what I'm writing. Tear drops mark the paper.

"Three goals," Kevin says, and he holds up three fingers. I want to poke his eyes out with my pen, but I keep scrawling, because I can't wait to get away from him.

When I finish, he looks at my paper and smiles. "Marcelle," he says brightly. "Fantastic. You can go to Group now." He immediately goes back to his iPad as if I were already gone.

"These are okay, then?" I ask.

"Since you ask, Marcelle, I'd say those are some piece-of-shit goals, but take them to the Group. James and the others will give you feedback. Maybe your peers will buy your bullshit, but I doubt it." I stand for a second in the doorway, stunned, not knowing whether to bolt for the exit or drag myself into Group for more abuse. I go to Group, not because I want to, but because the only thing that seems worse than going is trying to explain to Mom and Dad why I ran.

SEVENTEEN

I STARE DOWN the hall at the door to the Group room. There's a small window panel on the side of the door, and through it I can see the top of James's slightly bowed head. I try to breathe, counting my breaths, and by some miracle it sort of works. I breathe in and out. A few hot tears still run down my cheeks, but I'm not making a sound as I reach for the door handle.

I can't panic.

James, Cyndi, Ali, Maria, and Martin sit around the worn wood table. They have their journals open, all of them the same regulation black-and-white composition books, like the one I've left in my cubby. Martin is eating a doughnut and drinking coffee. I've hardly eaten anything since breakfast, and the sight of Martin's doughnut makes me feel faint. Cyndi, I notice as I work my way around to my seat, has a sandwich in front of her. She sees me look at her and gives me a tight smile. It's the sort of look that tells me she's making an effort to be nice, not that she actually likes me. "Here, take half," she says. Before I can say no, she's sliding half the sandwich over to me on a paper napkin. I say thanks too quietly for anyone to hear, and then James gets up and goes to the back of the room, where there's a small fridge. "Coke, Sprite, or Diet?" he asks. I say Sprite, since too much caffeine this time of day will probably keep me up. The last thing I need is my mind racing all night, thinking about Hannah, and what might happen next. Each hour Hannah stays missing I feel slightly more numb. I tell myself, there is nothing I can do, not now at least. Right now, I need to be here, in Group, not fucking this up.

"Okay," James says, glancing at the clock. "It's four already. We only have ninety minutes." Ninety minutes, an hour and a half, is an eternity. I think how long it will take me to get home for my bike and then back to Michiko's. Can I get to Michiko's by six to have at least a half hour with Andy before my parents get suspicious?

"I'd like to start," Cyndi announces. She sits up straight with her hands folded in front of her, like a grade-school kid giving a report, only she speaks in a voice that's way too loud for the size of the room, like she's talking to a hundred people, instead of just the five of us.

"So, I'm going college visiting with the step-monster," she says. "Yeah, I know, bad attitude, but you have to cut me some slack, because I need my boundaries with this bitch. I mean, I need to acknowledge she is who she is—a total gold digger, and that's the situation, and I have to accept it."

I wait for someone to interrupt her and tell her she can't talk like that in Group, but it doesn't happen. Everyone just nods. It's weird that Cyndi had her six-monther yesterday, but still seems to need to dominate everything today. Maybe she's just your typical attention whore after all.

Cyndi continues, "I have to figure out how to handle all this because, you know, there's my past with her and I have to be accountable." Cyndi goes through every detail of her college trip, down to whether she should help her stepmom pay for gas out of the money she has saved up from working at a retail store in Greenwich. My legs start to twitch. I'm supposed to present my goals today. I need to be formally accepted to the Group by submitting my goals and my accountability letter.

Conditional acceptance at the Center is almost immediate; you get through intake and you're in. But to be an actual member, you need to have your goals and plans accepted and to present your accountability letter to the Group. Until I get my act together about the accountability letter, my attendance at meetings doesn't even count toward my six-month rehab course. After I get my Sixer, like Cyndi, I can choose whether or not to attend Group. But as of now, it's like my three alcohol-free weeks are meaningless. I'm nowhere until I have unconditional acceptance.

"You should pay her for gas," Ali says to Cyndi, "but let your stepmom pay for the hotel rooms, because that'll be way too much, especially if she wants to stay in bougie places." I've zoned out, and when I snap to, I involuntarily shoot Ali a look. He frowns back at me. I can't believe they're all taking this crap of Cyndi's seriously.

"Have you written anything yet for your sober living contract?" James interrupts. "Are you limiting your search to schools with sober communities?" I tap my feet and sip my Sprite. I stare at the clock on the wall. I repress the desire to yawn. I'm both emotionally drained and jumpy. I want to scream that none of this matters. Who knows what Cyndi will be doing a year from now? Even if she has a plan, who knows if she'll follow it? It's like when I'm on a diet thinking about what I'll look like when it's over, but then it's never over, because it hardly even starts. I can see why it matters to Cyndi that she made it through her first six months, but I don't understand why all these other details of her life should matter to the rest of us.

It matters that people disappear. It matters that people are not found. My head throbs every time I think about the past twenty-four hours.

Cyndi nods. "I'm in touch with lots of sober student groups on Facebook," she says. "There are healthy living options at all my choices. No way I'm rooming with some stoner chick or some Adderall junkie." She shakes her head and grins. Again, I see the Hannah-like look—the hardness in her eyes, the flash of unexpected anger. You can see in Cyndi's straight little nose, the light blue eyes, the high cheekbones, the sort of girl her parents must have thought she'd be. Without tattoos and the crazy hair, she'd be a yacht-club type, a summers-in-Maine girl. But the girl she is doesn't need drugs to show herself. There is something combustible in Cyndi. I wonder without drugs what she uses to cool that fire. I see her glance at Martin, who has added nothing to the conversation. Yesterday, they had seemed close, but today he is disengaged and sullen. I wonder if that's her thing—playing the guys against each other. Today, it's James who seems to be winning her flirty glances, her nods, her long, deep looks.

Finally, Cyndi scribbles a few notes in her journal. "Thanks for your suggestions," she says. "These are great ideas. The money is really important for my family since I basically blew through half my college fund." Then she turns and looks straight at me. "I stole from my stepmom, you know. About fifty grand." I feel my jaw drop. I can't imagine how she pulled this off. A part of me feels like she's almost bragging, exaggerating even, for shock value—like Cyndi wants to make sure she's the biggest badass of us girls in Group.

"She hardly noticed it was missing, she's such a dumb, rich bitch. But I see now how fucked up I was."

James clears his throat. He seems impressed with Cyndi's magnanimity.

"It's pretty amazing what you've done in the last six months," James says. "I just want to give you props on the whole traveling-with-Becky thing. When you got here, you couldn't be in a room together." Cyndi looks meltingly at James.

"Just taking it a day at a time," Cyndi says, and smiles electrically.

I think how terrified I'd be to get Cyndi as a college room-mate, sober or not.

There's a heavy silence as Martin, Ali, Maria and I all eye one another, waiting for someone to start next. Martin runs his hand across his close-cropped head. My throat still feels dry. I'm not sure if I'm allowed to start speaking to introduce my goals. I think there may be a protocol I was supposed to read up on in the manual—some way to signal to James that I'm ready. But just as I get my courage up, Ali breaks the silence.

"I've been having trouble getting focused on school," Ali says. "I haven't been gaming, but I can't sit still. I'm, like, all over the house, bugging my brother and shit, anything instead of homework." I'm instantly sympathetic, but to my surprise Cyndi and James look stone-faced.

"I don't want to have a Group on this again, Ali," Cyndi interrupts, her face a white mask of annoyance. I'm amazed how quickly she goes from sunny and flirty to out-and-out bitchi-ness. "I feel like instead of changing, you're just talking about change. It's really frustrating." Ali suddenly looks small and miserable.

"I know," Ali says, grabbing both sides of his head. "I know, I know." To my astonishment, he seems to accept getting beat up on. Then James adds, "If you know, why don't you change? This is serious, Ali. Maybe you don't want to be here? Maybe you don't need Group or the Center if change is not on your agenda?" My heart skips a beat. I can't believe James has given him this ultimatum.

Ali looks close to tears. It's scary to see such a big kid about to cry. It's bizarre how James and Cyndi seem to be able to do and say whatever they want.

"I have to think about your feedback," Ali says. "But this is my issue, I guess. I really miss it. I miss gaming and weed so fucking much. I'm so pissed I can't concentrate. I just want to fucking hit something." He shakes his head and scowls. I can feel myself involuntarily nodding. Ali is the first person to say anything in this room that sounds like my life.

James looks around the table incredulous. "Ali, I can't believe I'm hearing this from you," he says. James's jaw is set. He stares for what seems like several minutes without blinking. I wonder if I'm seeing some fragment of the old James, a flash of the junkie, the kid who had no fear of the needle.

Cyndi suddenly laughs, a cold, incredulous bark. "It's really fucking unbelievable. You leave the building right after Group, when you could do all your work right here. This agitation you're crying about is something you've *pursued*." She says this last word with strange emphasis, as though it holds a secret meaning. How does anyone pursue agitation or anger?

"Everyone leaves after Group," Ali whines. Ali is now crying big, fat man-tears. He wipes them away impatiently, trying to recover, but he's dissolved into a snotty mess.

"Has Ali ever asked you to hang out?" Cyndi addresses James. James frowns and shakes his head. "Ali, when I first started here, I asked James to stay after Group almost every night. And he did. We'd watch TV, do our work together, listen to music. Sometimes I just sat and cried." Cyndi, like James, fixes Ali with a furious stare. It seems like something they've agreed between themselves to do, and I start to feel even more nervous. Have Cyndi and James been told to bully us? To befriend people one day and slaughter them the next? Is this part of the program somehow? Or is it something they've devised on their own?

"I hear Ali," Martin interjects, and I breathe a sigh of relief. Maybe there's at least one other sane person at the table, some-one who will actually stand up to James and Cyndi. "No one told me we could hang out here late," he adds. I notice for the first time that Martin speaks with a slight lisp and works hard to pronounce every word precisely.

I begin to think the remainder of Group will go this way, with James and Cyndi taking on Ali and Martin, me sitting here nervously, and Maria mutely staring into space.

Then James interrupts, retaking control. "I think this Group on Ali's procrastination issue has turned into a Group on goals in general and the function of peer leaders, which is probably a really good thing. I think we are all ready for a learning moment." James turns to me. I get a sinking feeling in my gut.

"I think if anyone here knows what the primary action a person on goals needs to make, we need to make that clear—Marcelle?" I shake my head and look away. Maria gazes at me, and I think I see the slightest smile cross her lips—is she laugh-ing at me, or is she shyly showing some sign of solidarity?

Cyndi looks impatient and I pray she doesn't speak. Martin sighs and looks at the ceiling, blinking. "We *pursue* our goals," Martin says. He says this bitterly, but James smiles approvingly.

"Right. Pursuit is active. That's how we work on our goals. We think about our pursuit all the *fucking* time. We move on from goals when we're thinking about them all the *fucking* time, not when we've stopped, not when it becomes easy, but when we know how hard it actually is every fucking day." James stops. He seems almost choked up, and everyone, even Cyndi, stares, captivated.

"That's why you guys have to ask questions. *Pursue.* You're too lonely or angry or bored at home, say so. Maybe you, Ali, have the wrong goal?" He pauses and looks around the room. I watch his Adam's apple rise and fall. James no longer seems like one of us. It's like he's not a kid at all, but someone special, someone who somehow knows more than any of us about how to have a life.

"Maybe you shouldn't be working on procrastination, Ali, or giving up gaming? Maybe you're overlooking what you need in your life because you're so blinded by having to push away what you can't let yourself have?

"I think you basically need more love, man. You need to surround yourself with love. That was someone's goal last year, right? 'Surround myself with loving friends.' I think that was Carrie. A really beautiful goal." Ali has stopped crying, and sits with his head down, nodding slowly. Just when I was convinced of James's total assholery, he starts talking to Ali about love.

I glance at the yellow pad where I've scribbled down my own goals. I doubt James will find much beauty in them.

"Let's have it. You're up." James turns his gaze to me.

I clear my throat. I take a deep breath and then blurt out some approximation of what I've written on Kevin's legal pad.

"Goal one is do all homework. Two is be more honest. Three is earn back Mom's and Dad's trust." I pause, suddenly wishing I had written more. "That's it. That's all," I say. Martin looks down at his hands. I am met by the blank stares of the others. I think I must have forgotten something, some critical word or catchphrase.

"I've actually really been struggling," I say hesitantly. "There's this thing with Hannah. It's starting to seem serious." I want them to see how afraid I am, and how I am not using Hannah as an excuse to not have my goals and plan completed.

They all stare in silence.

Then Cyndi lets out a big sigh. "This is tough," Cyndi says, "because I don't know you, but I have to say, Marcelle, I don't believe a word you say. I'm so sorry, but to me you sound like every addict I've ever met. This drama with your friend, Hannah?" She shakes her head, at a loss for words. "I'm not buying it." Everyone—even Martin, even Maria—nods. I feel like I've been punched in the stomach. I want to scream. This isn't fair. I'm telling the truth!

"Yeah." Martin shakes his head, scowling. "You remind me of where I was, like, a month or so ago." Everyone nods. Martin is the most recent kid to join Group besides me. "I mean, the accountability letter is not even something I know how to talk about. How do you have goals without at least doing a draft of that? This Hannah shit is smoke and mirrors in my book. Something you'd have known if you wrote your AL, or if you'd taken any of this seriously."

"That's true," Cyndi says. "I think you're on target, Martin, to question Marcelle's process. Your goals are really juvenile-sounding, really insubstantial." James nods sagely.

"Okay, I think it's actually not a great use of our time to do a Group on Marcelle's goals today," James says. "We all agree they're bullshit. Let's check back tomorrow. I think you should use the time to rework your goals, Marcelle. Come back to Group for a review when you've completed that step. Also, I think Martin is onto something with your AL. You need to get thinking about that as well. Could be clarifying." I nod, wiping away tears. The way James is talking makes me worried I'm somehow being demoted back to square one, like in some stupid little kids' board game where you think you're moving along, but then one roll of the dice and your progress is obliterated.

James brings the whole thing to a quick close. "So then, let's make Group time for Marcelle tomorrow. And Marcelle, I think the goals show that you are, like Cyndi says, still hiding from the truth. You're not being real with us, or yourself. So, you're still probationary. Not actually a part of this Group. You should take the rest of this afternoon to think on both your goals and your accountability letter, in whichever order you decide. That's our feedback, okay?"

At first, I'm too confused to move. Then, I slowly gather my things. Everyone watches me walk to the door. I'm not who they think I am, I tell myself. I know I'm better than this.

I hear James clear his throat as the door falls shut behind me. Maybe the Group will turn their attention to Maria now, Maria, whose ribs show through her red turtleneck, whose dark eyes bulge out of their sockets. How is she, Maria, more deserving than me, when she clearly continues to starve herself?

I get my school stuff out of my cubby, and throw myself onto one of the couches in the small lobby outside Kevin's office.

Kevin's door opens and he waddles out, a bunch of papers in one hand. When he sees me on the couch, he pauses, and raises his eyebrows in mock surprise. "Kicked you out, did he?" he asks. "That's good. You don't belong yet. Hope you get there, kid. This place and those jokers have a lot to offer you." I watch him do his fat-man shuffle down the hall to the small kitchen on the other side of the building.

"Fuck you," I mutter under my breath.

I look back at my blank journal page. I have to survive here; that's the bottom line. I read back through the goals I've written on the legal pad, and they really do sound pretty shallow after all. I hate to admit James was right. "Do all homework" is something a little kid would say. It's too small, and anyway, academics have always been my strength. I was doing most of my work even when I was hungover all the time.

Being more honest with Mom and Dad doesn't mean being honest in general. I have to *be honest.* I have to find some way to tell the truth about Hannah without destroying my own life.

It isn't that I have to earn Mom's and Dad's trust back, either. I have to *be trustworthy.* Mostly, I have to start trusting myself. I have to think about what I'm doing, so no one else gets hurt.

I jot down a new and improved list of goals: *focus on work, be honest, be trustworthy.* Honesty and trustworthiness seem like almost the same thing, but I know that for me, they're different.

These are the types of goals I can hold on to. I can pursue them, as James would say. Actually, I know if I don't, something else really bad might happen.

It's getting late and I'm tired, but I know I have to stick to my plan of meeting Andy at Michiko's. I'm not telling Mom and Dad about meeting Andy, but then again, no one has said I can't see Andy outside of school. Still, I feel my stomach tighten. I know what I'm about to do is wrong, and isn't about pursuing the goals I just wrote, but I know my life outside the Center isn't a place I can be totally honest and trustworthy about everything—not yet, anyway. At least if I can talk to Andy, maybe I'll have one person in my life I can trust who might also trust me.

I glance at the clock. I have fifteen minutes before Mom picks me up. I turn to a blank page in my journal and start my accountability letter. What Martin said isn't true, that I couldn't come up with good goals before I wrote my letter. Anyway, I know now what I have to say to Mom and Dad, and I know what I have to leave out. Hannah's story isn't my story. I didn't deal any drugs. I wasn't the one who went back to Alex's. I wasn't the one who went into that room, with the black sheet on the window, and stayed. Hannah has the kinds of secrets a girl would want to bury forever. I can tell my own story, and leave Hannah's secrets out of it.

EIGHTEEN

I SHUT THE car door and walk toward the garage. Mom stares after me. We hardly spoke the whole ride home from the Center. I dreaded that Mom would suggest dropping me at Michiko's and waiting for me to do my chores, but she seems to have forgotten all about my "job." "I've got to go over to Michiko's, remember?" I say. "Could you bring my bag in for me?" I make a show of taking Michiko's keys out of my book bag and putting them in the pocket of my overalls. Mom gives me a tight smile, meant, I suppose, to show her approval of my commitment to feeding Michiko's pets. At least she's not suspicious of why I'm so eager to go.

I pull my bike out of the garage. Fortunately, I still have the road bike Mom and Dad got me when they had the idea I'd ride for exercise—riding the reservoir loop road, like all the triathlon dads. But I'd stuck to the old fixed gear since the road bike's tires are too thin for the rock-strewn trails through the woods—the trails we actually use to get places. But now I have no choice but to clean the road bike off and ride awkward and hunched.

It's a short ride—four blocks, and then three streets over to Summit, where Michiko lives. The houses on my street are all pretty big, with long steps out front and backyards big enough for kids' games. Ours is a pea-green stucco with a big wrap-around porch and wide, stone pillars. Mom has a garden in back and pots of flowers all around the house in the summer. I glance back at the house as I ride away. It looks more than normal.

The ride is over too fast. I wish I could do a loop or ride the few blocks to CVS and get some candy, but I'm already freaking out about meeting Andy, and even something small like detouring into town seems too risky. I pull into Michiko's short, steep driveway. Her outside light has a sensor, which goes on as soon as I pull up to the house. I lean the bike against the garage, a few feet away from where my other bike died the night I crashed.

"Only a drunk could have survived that," the cop told my dad the night of the accident. I glance up into the woods toward the Death Wish path. It looks pretty in the semi-dark, with the red and yellow leaves glowing in the moonlight. "Is that what you're becoming?" Dad asked me in the morning at the hospital. "A drunk?"

I shook my head no. Everything hurt. But deep inside my bruised body was a part of me that had been unharmed by the accident, but crushed by Dad's question.

I turned away and cried into my pillow and Dad stroked my

hair lightly, but not for long. He didn't sit at my bedside or ask why I was crying. When he walked away his footsteps sounded heavy and quick.

Drunks, I wanted to say to him, *are craggy-faced, stink-breath old guys*.

I'm a girl, I wanted to say. *Just a girl.*

I have my key in Michiko's front-door lock when I suddenly have the unmistakable feeling I'm not alone. I'm half ready to scream when Andy steps out from behind the side of the house, near a single pine tree that is the exact shape and size of the perfect Christmas tree. I'm still shaking when he pats me on the shoulder and apologizes for scaring me.

"A normal person would have texted," I say once I've calmed down. "Who goes jumping out at people?" Andy shrugs and smiles in a funny, shy way. I'm expecting him to be hyped up and scared, too, but he seems happy to see me. I can feel Andy's closeness as he follows me into the house. *It's only Andy*, I tell myself—so why does my body feel like a tightly wound spring as I step into Michiko's gray-stone foyer and switch on the light?

I do everything I'm supposed to: feed Marco, who weaves between my legs as I dish out the fancy albacore tuna. I work my way through the spotless house into the living room, switching on the lights as I go. "She hates coming home to a dark house," I explain to Andy, but he doesn't say anything. He just runs his finger along my back, tracing the way my braid sits between my shoulder blades. It gives me the chills and I wriggle a little, but keep quiet. This is not us. We have never touched each other like this.

The bird sits in his nearly ceiling-high cage, squawking. "Oh bird," I whisper. "Shut the fuck up." Then I open the cage door and let him step onto my finger and then perch on my head, while I whistle "Mary's Got a Gun" and change his water. I feel him going from one clawed-foot to the other, pulling my hair as he steps. Andy watches, shaking his head. "Mr. Bird," I say, "meet Andy." I'm showing off a little, I know, but the bird and I are pretty good friends at this point, and "Mary's Got a Gun" is my addition to his song list.

"Andy," the bird says. "Andy, Andy."

"He knows his animal sounds, too," I say. And then the bird says "Meow," proving my point. I flush slightly.

"People are fucking weird," Andy says. "Keeping a bird like that, teaching it to say stupid things."

"Yeah, it's warped," I say. "But I like Michiko. She's not afraid to be different."

Andy looks thoughtful, and for a second I think he's going to start talking deep shit about himself, or about Jonas and the situation at home, but he just says, "Put that bird back in the cage, would you?" As I open the cage door and put the bird back in, Andy leans closer to me. The bird cocks his head, waiting, I know, for me to scratch him, but I shut and fasten the door of the cage.

We don't have a lot of time.

"I'm scared," I murmur. I start to cry a little. The tears come faster than I can wipe them away. Andy pulls me toward him and kisses me on the top of my head.

"I know," he says in a hoarse whisper, pulling me closer.

"What do you think about her phone?" I ask.

"I don't know. . . . Maybe it's nothing. Maybe she just dropped it?" Andy murmurs. He kisses me on the mouth now, and I kiss him back.

I thought I had told Andy to come to Michiko's so we could talk. But I don't clarify. I don't tell him what Mom said about the cops and their search.

Andy is two steps behind me on the stairs and catches up by stumbling, and then grabbing me around the waist. I flinch, because I'm not small where he's touching me, but Andy doesn't seem to care. I lead him down behind the stairs to Michiko's son's room. It smells of emptiness, of laundry detergent and furniture polish, of closed windows and still air.

I lie back on the scratchy red-and-black wool blanket that is still tucked in all around the edges. I feel a slight twinge of guilt as I kiss Andy again and he climbs on the bed next to me. We shouldn't be doing this, not here, not now, and the obviousness of this makes me want to laugh, but I know if I do I'll ruin everything, maybe forever, and so I somehow stifle it.

Andy's lips are full and dark, almost brown, but his face is small, delicate, like the rest of him. His stomach is rock-hard, and lifting his shirt I can see every one of his ribs. He's far too small for me, but I like his ink-dark eyes, and his girly thick lashes. I like the questioning, grateful way he looks at me. I like the silent, peaceful house around us and the almost-empty boy's room we're doing this in—the track trophy on the bookshelf, a kids' microscope, an old laptop on the built-in mini-desk— everything is still, relics of a recently discarded life. Being here reminds me that things won't always be like they are. We'll move on, somehow.

I kiss Andy harder to show him that I'm into what we're doing. I let him undo my overall buckles and slide his hand under my shirt. He feels around my back and undoes my bra with surprising skill. I think of all the other rooms in town like this one, rooms that have been left empty for real lives far from here, far from high school. It's not our fault that this room is here waiting for us.

Andy pulls away from me and rests on his elbow, his breath warm on my neck. His dark hair is still spiked on top and gelled smooth on the sides. The last time we hooked up was in the woods on the way home from Senna's. There had been stars out, and noise from the others in the garage, Chuck fooling around on his guitar, Hannah's high laugh.

"Andy?" I say. "I need to tell you something."

"Yeah?" he says. He stares at me with his big, dark eyes, and waits.

"I feel almost like we just met, or like we're just *starting* to know each other for real." I laugh nervously. "It's kind of like all that other stuff that happened over the summer doesn't even count. Does that sound crazy?"

There's a long, uncomfortable silence. Then Andy moves

over on the bed, and makes room for me right next to him. He turns my face to his, and kisses me on the lips. "Marci, I've liked you since eighth grade," he says softly. "You were the smartest kid in Ms. Billings's English class. Remember? You always got hundreds on all of her impossible vocab quizzes. You never raised your hand, but whenever she called on you, you had the answer. You were chill, quiet. You didn't wear makeup. You weren't loud, or mean, or gossipy. You didn't bother anyone, or make fun of anyone, or act like you were smarter than anyone. You were just you. The best girl."

I whisper into his shirt. "Oh my God. You're so ridiculous."

"I know," he says. "It's part of what got to me about us before. How it was all about being wasted. I still thought of you as that supersmart girl." He pauses and looks at the ceiling. "But then you stopped being her."

My heart sinks. I'm not sure what's happening. Why is Andy here with me, in Michiko's kid's abandoned bedroom, if this is how he feels? I breathe deeply. "I'm going to find her again," I say. "I think that's kind of what rehab is for."

"No," Andy says definitively. "She's gone."

I pull away and sit up, alarmed; he smiles and grabs my arm. "No, not like that. I don't mean it in a bad way. It's just, I had you on a pedestal or something. I didn't want you to do anything crazy or fucked up. I wanted you to be a kid still. That perfect girl. But then we were all fucking up, and I got confused, and I needed it to stop. I didn't want to hurt you. Not the little-kid you, or who I thought you were. *This* you. Because I like *this* you. Rehab-or-whatever you."

"I like you too," I say. "I like this, here tonight. I like being able to have a real conversation with you."

Andy is quiet for a minute. "You know that night at Alex's?" he asks.

"Yeah. Terrible fucking night," I say.

"I'm sorry," he says. "I told Hannah to find you, but I didn't do enough. I shouldn't have let you go off alone with all those fucked-up guys around."

"Jesus, Andy," I say. "Fucking Alex." I bury my face in his chest, and he strokes the back of my head. "Why did Hannah have to get involved with him?"

"I guess it's pretty much my fault," Andy says. "You know the webcam he has in that room at his place is just one he has set up for the girls he actually knows? He's got girls all over the county—girls with cameras in their own rooms. He has a network of these girls from the community college—friends of friends who want to make some money."

"Shit," I say. "I knew Alex was a dirtbag, but seriously? Fuck. What was Hannah thinking?"

"Well, Jonas is the one who set up the hosting system. Alex isn't that bright a guy. I didn't know about what Jonas was up to until Hannah got involved. Then he kind of freaked out, because she's underage and he knows her and everything. He saw it like there was this division—Alex dealt with the girls and he did the technology. But then Hannah got started, and Jonas couldn't really say that anymore. If my parents find out the kind of business Jonas is in, they'll disown him. I don't know what to do."

I rest my head on Andy's chest and he strokes my hair back from my forehead. I know it's getting late, and that my parents will go crazy if I stay out much longer, but I can't bring myself to leave.

"Andy," I say. "You know the cops are looking for her now. Out wherever they found her phone."

Andy pulls me close and speaks in a soft, low voice. "It's all over town, Marci. They found it out near Playland, by the beach there, on some nature trail. Jonas heard from a guy he knows in Port Chester. Some EMT guy." I'm surprised Andy has more details than I do. I try to picture the place he means. I've been out there before on class trips, on walks with my dad—and there was one time over the summer, I remember being in that parking lot late at night—one night we met up with Jonas and Alex, before spending the night at Senna's.

I lean against Andy's chest. "What do you think it means?" I ask. He picks up my braid and brushes the end against his hand, as though it were a paintbrush.

"Not sure," he says. "Jonas claims to know nothing, and he swears Alex never went near her, but I just don't know." We're both quiet, and then Andy leans over and kisses me again. The kiss lasts so long I wonder if we're going back where we started, but it's late, and eventually Andy pulls away.

"Let's get out of here, before Michiko gets home," I say.

Outside, it's gotten chilly, although it's still mild for fall.

Andy kisses me goodbye, then jogs around the back of the house where he's left his bike. I get on my own bike and head out onto the bumpy street. I miss my old, fat-tired fixed-gear. My hands are cold and my eyes tear in the wind, half-blinding me. All the houses I pass are lit up and look warm and welcoming, but soon they blur together, and all I see is the darkness ahead of me.

NINETEEN

THE NEXT DAY, I'm early for American Lit, and the classroom is almost empty, except for Chuck, who sits two rows over from me. Chuck stares at his copy of *The Scarlet Letter*, which reminds me I'm at least a chapter behind. He sees me come in, looks up, and nods, but then goes back to his reading. By some extraordinary stroke of luck, Ms. Callahan is in a departmental meeting, and we are getting the period to read. Mr. Walker, a semi-retired teacher, is the substitute. Walker is a nice guy and it's a smart-kid class, so people file in, look up at the board, get the picture, and start to read.

I haven't spoken to anyone since I saw Andy last night at Michiko's. When I got home, my parents had both finished eating and were working in their separate studies. Mom hadn't heard anything more from Elise Scott, and so it was a weirdly quiet night. Between the stress of being kicked out of Group, and running over to Michiko's to meet Andy, I barely had the energy to do my homework and get through half of my accountability letter before passing out from exhaustion.

I want to know what's happened with Senna, and whether the cops have questioned him, and whether he's still suspicious that I know something about what Hannah was doing Sunday night. I think if I can get Chuck to talk, I can put my mind at ease. But even after I move a row closer to him, Chuck keeps reading and underlining, his eyes lowered. He must feel my gaze on him, because he glances at me darkly, as though warning me off. I shake my head and give him a what-the-fuck stare, but he's back to his reading.

I spend the rest of the period freaking out about why Chuck is ignoring me, and I'm ridiculously relieved when he comes over to my desk as I pack up at the end of class.

"What's up?" he says. He sounds casual, but drums nervously on the corner of my desk. I shrug as I grab my iPad and notebook, not trusting myself to speak. I can't tell if he's deliberately messing with my head, or if he just wanted to get his work done during class. Either way, I can't shake the feeling that something is not right. Do he and Senna think I'll spill to my parents or the cops about the deal with Alex? I feel a shiver spread throughout my body, a feverish chill. *I can't cry*, I tell myself. *I can't visibly crack up.* Chuck and I head wordlessly to the cafeteria. I can't think of a thing to say to him to break the silence.

I have to get my head together to get through this endless day. I have a fifteen-minute break before History with Senna and Andy. I don't want to see Senna at all, and I wish I could see Andy alone.

Chuck doesn't have a break, but is getting provisions to bring to math. I hang with him on the cafeteria line, since it would be awkward to walk away, even though I'm just getting a tea and could slide by in the beverage-only line. "Hey, gorgeous," Elsa, the cafeteria server, says to Chuck. "What you having?" Chuck half smiles at her and points to a corn muffin, the kind with a sugary top. I pause behind him as Elsa places the muffin on a white paper plate and hands it to Chuck, who doesn't say thanks, or even look back in Elsa's direction. I can see the annoyance on her face and I blush, as though Chuck's rudeness was somehow my fault.

I decide I have nothing to lose by telling him what little news I have about Hannah—about her definitely not being at her dad's, or anywhere else Elise Scott can think of.

"Why would she go there?" Chuck says softly. "She hates her dad." This reminds me how Chuck and Hannah used to be, back before Senna stole her away last winter—the way Chuck would stare at her in the cafeteria and text her from every class.

It took one or two weekends at Senna's garage, with Senna taking Hannah aside and handing her his tiny glass vial. Back then, before Jonas hooked Senna up with Alex, Senna had a city connection. But it was inferior-quality blow, dealt by some kid Senna knew from Hackman, who likely cut his already-crap coke with corn starch. Still, Hannah liked the buzz, and the coolness of being singled out by Senna; everyone knew Senna's stash was precious, and that having it set him apart from all the other Waverly kids, even the other druggy guys, who mostly ordered fake pills online, or bought dirt-tasting weed from some guy in New Rochelle.

"I know," I say. "I guess it was just her mom's first thought." But then I take a chance and add, "I actually thought it made sense, if someone was looking for her around here, and she got scared." My voice comes out weirdly muffled, like I'm afraid to hear my own words.

Chuck waits for the cashier lady to ring him up. I think how clean-cut he looks: button-down, Top-Siders, all his clothes neat, even the pants weirdly wrinkle-free, like he'd had them dry-cleaned. No one would peg Chuck for a cokehead. But he's gotten almost as bad as Senna and Hannah. In fact, watching Chuck there in the cafeteria line, I wonder if he's a little wired; he's fidgety, and seems to be grinding his teeth. He's so pale and thin, still hot, but maybe bordering on too thin. His tan cords fall below the hip, bunch under his dark leather belt, and bag around his legs.

"I don't know," Chuck says. "Do you know everyone Hannah knows? Maybe someone's letting her hang out . . ." Chuck pauses as he walks toward the cafeteria door, opens a milk container, and drinks. Then he adds four heavy-sounding words: ". . . until things calm down."

But Chuck doesn't say anything more, and I'm afraid to press. He doesn't say a word about Senna. When he says things need to "calm down," is he talking about the coke-dealing Senna is still doing, or about the webcam stuff Hannah was doing with Alex? I'm not sure if Chuck knows more than I do, or even less.

Chuck thrusts his muffin at me, and I hold the plate while he stuffs his remaining, unopened milk into the side pocket of his book bag. I hand the muffin back and am about to ask him one last question, when he turns with a wave of his hand. I watch him stroll toward the door. He looks like one of those actors who's way too old, too poised to be in high school, but there he is, playing the part of the suave junior guy, hair falling in perfect, loose waves, jaw too square to be for real.

Then, to my shock, Chuck turns back and returns to where I'm standing, like a loser.

"Marcelle," he says, clearing his throat and looking down at his feet. "I was meaning to ask how it's going with you. At that place?" He looks up and stares hard right at me, like he suddenly cares deeply about my sobriety, something I've hardly spoken to anyone about.

"You mean the Center?" I ask, startled.

"Yeah," he says.

"It's okay," I say. But of course it isn't, and I decide to take a stab at honesty. "Actually, it's fucking hard." He nods, taking it in, but he still doesn't walk away. I have five minutes to get to class, just enough time if I leave now and walk fast, but Chuck is looking at me with those piercing eyes—at *me* and no one else. It's like he wants answers—real answers, and he thinks, for some reason I can't imagine, that I have them.

"It's just that I've been thinking about doing something like that," he says. Then he adds, "It's not like you're the only one." He shoves his hands in the front pockets of his pants. The waistband falls slightly and a narrow band of taut torso is exposed. I am Jell-O, despite all the warning bells going off in my brain. Even if I could have him, Chuck is ten thousand times more trouble than he's worth. These are the things I tell myself to try to steady my brain. I forget, just for a second, all about Andy.

I get my focus back, at least temporarily. I'm not sure what Chuck wants me to do—if he wants to come with me to the Center or just to talk about rehab. The truth is any of the rest of them could have, should have, ended up like me. I'm just the pathetic one who got caught. Being a cokehead is easier to conceal than being a drunk. Fits in your pocket. Doesn't make you puke.

It makes sense Chuck would reach his breaking point now, with Hannah missing and Senna getting worried about his and Hannah's connection with Alex. If I were Senna I'd be afraid to make a move. I can see why Chuck is freaking out, too—he's maybe out of drugs and too scared to find any, looking for anything to get him through—even getting sober.

But then I get a paranoid idea. I glance at Chuck and he looks down and away, anywhere but at me, and my heart skips about five beats. He looks pale and nervous, like there is something more he wants to say.

I breathe deeply and let the thought fully form. This is something Senna has put Chuck up to in order to keep me quiet at the Center, and to keep his connection to Alex from surfacing. Senna thinks I'm telling them everything there, and that the Group kids will talk, or that they'll tell me I need to spill my guts to Elise Scott and the cops. He's worried he'll get busted, not just for dealing, but for Hannah being Alex's webcam bitch. I don't know exactly what's an actual crime and what isn't, but porn plus drugs seems pretty criminal.

Chuck could be Senna's spy.

It's too fucked up to be true, but then again it's not. Senna and Chuck, even Andy—all of them have something to hide. None of my friends need me blabbing about the kind of shit that was going on with Hannah, and I'm the only one with nothing to lose. Andy and I agreed we need to wait it out—if Hannah comes back and we've ratted, her life in Waverly is over. But if Hannah's in some kind of danger—if she's not coming back, and no one seems to know where she's gone—what then? I don't even know Alex's last name. I'm not sure I could say where his apartment even is. I was wasted when I went there. I know enough to get my friends in trouble, but that's basically all.

There was that afternoon in the first week of the school year, when Hannah showed me the schoolgirl skirt and the long black wig, and gave me the details. She said she'd never have to do anything for real, no actual sex, but Alex already had her on camera five or six times. "He's got these older girls from the college doing all kinds of shit with each other, with guys. It's some sick shit. I just have to take off my sweater, hike up the skirt, and listen to these guys tell me how beautiful I am; it's pathetic. Alex says I can make more than five hundred a month. It's two months, and I can almost double that with the coke I can sell with Senna. I don't even look like me, Marce, admit it," she said. It was like the wig made all the difference, like once she put it on, she was no longer Hannah Scott. She almost had me convinced that it could be that easy.

"Marcelle?" Chuck says. "You going to answer me? I kind of got to know."

As usual, Chuck is unreadable. But I have no choice. I have to seem like I believe that he wants help. There is nothing else for me to do, nothing else that makes sense. "You should check it out. It's not for everyone, but at least it's close," I say finally. I barely get the words out, and I can see Chuck can tell I'm not enthusiastic. "You don't need an appointment. You go down there the first time and fill out a bunch of intake forms with a parent. Then there's a meeting with a counselor. That's when they eviscerate you. Then, you get to come to Group, and die a little every day."

"Yeah," he says, ignoring my attempt at humor. "I think I'll take a look." My heart is in my throat as he walks away.

I'm being paranoid. Chuck could just want to get sober. He's been using nearly as much as Hannah, and clearly has lost a lot of weight. Still, I can't imagine the Center would be someplace anyone would *want* to go. I was *sent* to the Center. It was Dr. Hagan who told me and my parents that the Center was the best place in the county for a truly fucked-up kid. He used those words: *truly fucked up*.

TWENTY

I HALF LISTEN to Mr. Kaufman, taking down what he types on his laptop, which appears simultaneously on the smartboard. But I'm distracted, not by Andy, who's sitting in front of me, and whose broad shoulders are close enough to touch, but by the feeling that I'm being watched.

I glance over my shoulder and see Senna, his narrow, gray eyes closed to half slits. He slumps at his desk, hands in the pockets of his huge hoodie, not even pretending to take notes. When I turn, he stares directly at me and does not look away. I open my hands in a what-the-fuck gesture, and Mr. Kaufman sees me. "Up here, Marcelle. Here's where all the action is." I hear someone scoff, but I'm afraid to turn around again. This is a warning, I tell myself.

Andy waits for me outside after class. I stand next to him but don't say anything. Even through my fear, I feel a warmth just being near Andy. For a minute, neither of us moves, then Andy reaches over and picks up a loose curl from my shoulder and twirls it around his finger. I feel shaky in the knees.

But then Senna walks over, as if we're waiting for him.

"Hey," I say to Senna. "Heard anything?" Senna shakes his head, takes out a piece of gum, unwraps it, and pops it in his mouth. The sweet gum smell seems to fill the hallway.

"Her dad's here," Andy interjects flatly. "I saw him this morning with her mom, going into the main office." Senna scoffs again like he did in class. But he doesn't look at Andy. He looks at me.

"You know, it's not like she's going to *want* to come back if people are talking shit about her," Senna says. He peers over my shoulder like he sees someone, but when I look there's no one there.

"Don't look at me," I say. "One more whisper about any shit I did, didn't do, or knew about, my ass is off to some boot camp. You have no idea how close my parents are to sending me away to real rehab. Last thing I would do is say anything that would get *her* in trouble." I feel in my gut this is the right thing to say. I've been busted—why would I want to bring more shit down on myself?

Andy shakes his head. Senna shifts his mostly empty-looking book bag from one arm to the other and nods like he gets it. I think he actually looks reassured, which scares the fuck out of me, since it means I'm probably right—that he's been worried about what I've been saying about Hannah at the Center.

"Well, Marce, you be sure to give a shout-out when you

hear from her, all right?" Senna commands, rocking back on his heels. I nod. It's weird the way he seems to have established me as the contact person, as though there is some kind of plan at work, and Hannah is going to be in touch. I still don't know whether Senna's thinking that Hannah ran away is based on something he knows, or something he wants to believe.

As we watch Senna lumber down the hallway, Andy squeezes my hand. "You okay?" he asks.

"Yeah," I say. "Thanks. Scared out of my mind, but I guess other than that, I'm okay."

"I know," Andy says. "We'll talk in gym, okay?" Andy and I have gym together after lunch. It's not awful—he looks decent in shorts with his soccer-player legs, but it's still awkward, since handball is coed. For some reason I can't understand, and that Coach Stevens certainly does not get, I am the queen of handball. No one touches me. It's one of those gifts you realize you have one day, only it's random and useless. It's like the saddest freebie the universe could ever grant.

Andy pulls me close, and gives me a quick hug. Then he whispers in my ear, "Don't be afraid, Marci. Don't be afraid."

Andy knows I have every reason to be scared, and so does he; it's why he insists I shouldn't be—people always feel the need to say the useless things twice.

TWENTY-ONE

AT LUNCH, I decide to lie low in the library. Or that's my plan, anyway, until I see Ms. Grant in the hall. "Just the girl I need," she says with a fake-sounding cheerfulness. "I was about to make a PA announcement to call you to the office, so we're both in luck."

I stare. "A meeting with Hannah Scott's folks," Ms. Grant says in a low, sympathetic voice. "I'm sure you're as concerned as they are. Spoke to your mom as well, and she's on her way. Just come with me, sweetheart." My vision goes in and out of focus, and for a second I'm afraid I may faint. I try to breathe, and at first my breath is so shallow I think I'll hyperventilate. I need to stay calm. I need to think. I follow Ms. Grant across the green to the office on wobbly legs.

I don't see any police cars in front of the office like last year when stupid, zit-faced Connor Eliot called in a fake bomb threat. But I do see my mom pull into a space in the front row of the staff lot marked *For Emergency Pickup Only*. My heart drops. I shiver. The sky has darkened, with some heavy-looking clouds looming directly overhead. It's as though the seasons have changed within the hour.

There's something coming together in front of me, something I should be able to see, but can't. I can only see these parts: Elise Scott and Hannah's dad, Alan, who I only recognize because he's sitting near Elise at the table inside the family conference room; Senna and Chuck skulking around the office door, looking down at their feet, out the window, anywhere but directly at another person; Andy by the meeting room entrance, like he's waiting for me, hands in his pockets, hair matted down in front, as though he has hastily mashed the spiky parts.

I follow Ms. Grant and her clicky-clacky heels into the conference room. Everyone else follows behind. I stare straight ahead at Ms. Grant's smooth bun and thin silver hoops. Ms. Grant is young, maybe not even thirty, but she tries hard to look serious and different from us, when only ten years ago she *was* us. She probably thought being a guidance counselor would be all about college essays and kids crying in her office about their breakups. I bet she never thought how she would handle a real problem, a problem like a missing girl.

Elise Scott sits at the table in the guidance office across from Dr. Henry, the principal. Elise is wearing her usual bright-red lipstick, but her face is a mess. Her eyes and cheeks are red and puffy, and her mouth quivers, like she's holding back a giant, room-filling sob. Alan has dark, charcoal-like circles under his eyes. I sit next to him after Ms. Grant pulls out a chair for me, and I think I can smell the fear on him, a sharp, musty odor.

Mom must have made a call from the car, because she comes in at about one o'clock, at least ten minutes after I saw her pull into the parking lot; she sits at the other end of the table from me, where there are a few empty seats. She eyes me briefly, breathes deeply, then focuses on Dr. Henry.

Dr. Henry looks like World War Three has broken out and he's president. His fat cheeks have a wobble to them that is sometimes funny to watch, but now it just reminds me how sad old people can look.

Then two cops in uniform walk in, and another guy with a big chest and shoulders, who I assume must be a detective. The uniform guys are the usual youth officers; I've seen them around—a dark-haired, maybe-Hispanic guy and an African-American woman with massive hands. They're the same cops who come to school every time someone gets busted with weed and they want to scare the rest of us, only this time they look hyped. The detective is very blond, with blond eyelashes and eyebrows.

I sit wishing there were something I could do to brace myself. It's like the seconds before you know for sure you're going to be in a crash. Or like on a rollercoaster, when you're freaking out, but it's far too late to change your mind; you're way up at the top of the ride—nothing to see but unending blue sky; your mouth is already preparing to scream, your throat opening wide, taking in a huge, suffocating breath.

I want to be strapped in. I want to not fall.

When Dr. Henry speaks, the cops all simultaneously look at their hands, even the Rice-Krispies-looking detective guy, as though they were school kids and he was their principal. "As all of you know, our student Hannah Scott has been missing since Sunday night. Her mother apprised us of this fact, and the initial thought was that Hannah ran away, possibly to her father's house. There is, however, reason to believe that this is not the case." Dr. Henry hesitates, shoots a look at Mr. Scott, who's face is like a gray, crinkled mask. The guy looks like a zombie, frozen in a moment of horrible incomprehension—*No, it's not possible*, the face says. *This is not real.*

Dr. Henry continues. His voice is not his usual loudspeaker drone, but weighty with his own disbelief at what he has to say. "These are the officers who are working to find Hannah Scott. It is thought by all of us here that you, Marcelle, Robert, Charles, and Andrew, might, in the company of staff and parents, help in this initial meeting with the police. Especially you, Marcelle, as Hannah communicated with you shortly before she went missing."

Everyone turns and looks my way. I flush and begin to sweat. But they look at me without anger. They are all wide-eyed with what seems like hope, like somehow I, Marcelle Cousins, teen fuck-up, might have some important knowledge, some information that will save the day. I squirm guiltily beneath their collective gaze.

The room is quiet as the door to the conference room opens

once more and in walks Mrs. Glasser, looking very thin in a black skirt and top, and Andy's mom, a small, attractive Indian woman, with red lipstick and a glossy ponytail. The only one without a parent at the meeting is Senna, which hardly comes as a surprise, since his parents never show up anywhere. I watch as Andy gives his mother a slight wave.

I think back on Sunday night. Have I forgotten anything? What do I have to add to the story? Hannah often stayed out late. But something felt different this time. There was something strange about her texting me—something uncharacteristic about her asking me to lie. Usually, when Hannah does something wild, she doesn't draw me in; she doesn't need to. Like with the webcam for Alex—she said nothing until the thing was done. The wig and the other sex-toy crap she got—she did that on her own, or with Senna. She didn't ask me what I thought. She never asked for my help.

"This is an opening of an investigation, a collection of facts that we as a staff, together with friends and family, must supply to the police," Dr. Henry continues. Everyone at the table nods, including the cops.

Dr. Henry looks down at some imaginary papers, pauses, and says, "Elise, if you could please . . ." But then he stops and stares at Elise Scott and her bulgy eyes, as though doubting the woman's ability to speak. I almost cry just looking at her, but she swallows once or twice and then starts speaking in a surprisingly clear voice. I glance at Chuck, Senna, and Andy. Chuck and Senna both stare into their laps, but Andy sits up very straight and looks directly at me. His eyes are round with fear.

"Thanks, everyone," Elise starts. "Well, I guess I should say what needs to be said. That is, we have been extremely worried about Hannah, not since Sunday, but for a long time." My mother stares at Elise, nodding her agreement.

Hannah's mom continues. "I have been very concerned since Sunday night, but the police have made a discovery that has made us . . ." She breaks off, and Alan reaches across the table for the hand he can't touch. ". . . a discovery that has placed us in a situation no parents—no one, really—should ever be in." She pauses and wipes her eyes with a tissue she holds crumpled in her hand. She takes a deep breath.

"As many of you already know, the police have found Hannah's cell phone. The last time her phone was used was Sunday and this was to text Marcelle. The police are now ready to release the information that the phone was found near Playland Amusement Park, in the nature preserve. It was found in some reeds off the path by a dog walker." Elise Scott stops at the word *walker*, as though somehow this is too much. She drops her head and continues. "The police have now ascertained that the phone has more than one set of fingerprints on it. One set is obviously Hannah's. But it appears that someone else also used her phone. It appears from preliminary tests on the prints that the person had been using drugs. There are trace amounts of cocaine on Hannah's phone."

At first Elise's body shakes and no sound comes out. When

the sound comes, it's terrible. I'm so startled by the fact that a woman can make a sound like Elise Scott makes that I have no reaction to the news, and no thought about what it could mean.

I try to focus on something other than Elise Scott's inhuman wail. But then I see my mom staring at me from across the table. She, too, is shocked. She stares, it seems, without comprehension, as though I'm not her daughter but some new frightening piece of a story that has just become a thousand times more horrible than it was. I absorb the fact that something terrible is happening and the people in this room think that I might know why. An abyss has opened up and taken Hannah. I'm halfway engulfed in that abyss myself. I glance around the table. They watch me dangle. Both Senna and Chuck meet my gaze. I can never tell what Senna is thinking. But Chuck is clearly falling apart. I remember back when Chuck and Hannah were together. I remember how she would sometimes grab him by the strap of his book bag, and lead him wherever she wanted to go.

Dr. Henry interrupts Elise Scott. "What we and Hannah's family would like from all of you," he says, eyeing each of the kids at the table, "is for you to know that any information you can give the police is critical at this time. If any of you know who Hannah was with last Sunday night, you must come forward immediately. You need to tell Detective Perez what you know."

The room is silent, except for the sound of Elise Scott crying. I don't know who Hannah was with or where she went. I can't answer the question. She told me nothing. They don't understand. I lost Hannah. I don't know when. But we all lost each other. Everybody did. At Senna's, we were all alone.

My mom's face has turned pale. Her lips quiver. Her brow is a network of deep creases. I want to tell her to stop looking that way, but they are all doing it. Every adult in the room has crumpled. The air is thick with their misery. The only people who resemble normal human beings are the cops, and they scan our faces stonily, waiting for one of us to start talking.

I slow my breath, breathing deeply, but I can't slow my racing mind. I struggle to piece together the facts. I already knew that Hannah's cell phone was found. Elise told me and my parents that Monday night. Andy knew basically where it was found. But now the cops have revealed something about a set of fingerprints. What are they saying? Someone had Hannah's phone? Do they think one of us knows who?

"Marcelle?" my mom begins, her voice thin and raspy. "Marcelle, do you know any reason Hannah might be out there? Anywhere near that place? Was this a hangout of yours? A place people were getting high?" My mom falters on the word *high*. Facts are stacking up for Mom, too—facts like *This could have been you, Marcelle.*

I shoot my mom a look. I want to tell her I'm not to blame. What happened to Hannah could not have happened to me. That much I do know. I wasn't her.

But Hannah's problems are mine now. That's what this meeting is about—the school and the cops telling all of us to get our acts together, and tell them everything we know. I glance toward the guys. Chuck gazes blankly at the white tabletop. Senna stares at the ceiling. Andy looks down at his lap. Will he spill about Jonas? Where will that lead?

My heart beats out of my chest. My palms sweat. I don't know where to turn. I keep losing my train of thought, my sense of time, where I am.

"No, no," I say, but my voice comes out strange, and I shake my head rapidly for emphasis. I try to think about this place, the nature preserve, near Playland. I know it well. You can see the Dragon Coaster from there, and the old flume ride they had to close after some stoned kid climbed out of the fake-log thing and drowned. When had I been there last? It was early in the summer, but I was drunk. Shit-faced. Puking out the window of a car. Jonas's car. Or was that somewhere else? Some other night? They want to know what I know, not what I don't know, not what I can't remember.

I shake my head again. "I don't know why she would be there," I finally say, and my voice is clear, recognizable. I need more air. *Yes*, I tell myself. *Breathe*. I try to think of how to say what I know. How do I tell a story that will make sense to these people? But this is not my story. I am only Marcelle. I'm not that important.

"But the young lady texted you, did she not?" the detective asks. My mom shoots him a look, then glances back at me, and I can tell she is not okay with this; she does not like the cop addressing me directly, no matter how furious she is with me, no matter how disappointing I am.

It doesn't matter anymore. I've been found out. I'm a bad person, not the kind of bad person who hurts people on purpose, but some other kind of bad—careless bad, apathetic bad, weak bad. There is nothing left to do but admit this fact.

"Yes, I got a text Sunday. I told my mom. I told her mom." I nod toward Elise Scott. I did that one small thing right.

The detective looks at my mom. He clears his throat and purses his lips. "We're going to need to see your daughter's phone, and to ask her some additional questions." He glances my way and then holds Mom's gaze steadily. My mom doesn't miss a beat. She hands the guy her business card. She's switched gears into Professional Lawyer Mom mode.

"You can be in touch with me later today," she says. The detective looks back at me now, not unkindly, but with the sort of penetrating interest that makes me feel like it would be wrong not to talk to him.

Mom is an estate lawyer, not a criminal lawyer, but I know she won't let the cop ask me anything more. Just the other day she read an article in the *Times* about some kids in the nineties who had given false confessions to the police and ended up in prison for ten years for crimes they didn't commit. *That's insanity*, she had said. *It's insanity to let a child speak to the police.* She had shaken her head in disbelief. *Children*, she kept saying, though it was clear from the article they were teenagers, and not little kids.

My chest hurts and my head throbs. Everyone around me looks odd, almost frozen in place. I'm too scared *not* to say anything. If Mom only cares about protecting me, if all anybody cares about is protecting their own kids, who will protect Hannah? Elise and Alan surely can't help her on their own.

The sound of my own voice surprises me. It's like a recording or something I'm listening to on TV.

"Hannah was involved with people," I say, and pause. I have their attention now; everyone leans forward. I can hear Alan Scott breathing next to me, his mouth open wide, like the mouth of a baby in the face of a grown man. Senna continues to stare at the ceiling.

"Drug people. From White Plains," I say. The adults look at me blankly, as though I were speaking a foreign language. All around me are unblinking eyes, eyes that tell you nothing but that you are in big shit. No mercy. No understanding. "Cocaine people," I add, trying to sound more technical. Then, suddenly, the silence around the table feels less cold, less empty. I sit up taller. Deep down, in my gut, I know I'm doing the right thing, at last.

"I actually don't know any of them well. Just this one guy, Alex. I don't even know his last name." I add this probably too quickly, since it sounds even to me like I'm covering my own ass. I pause and shut my eyes for a millisecond. I try to remember how it is you can tell when someone is telling the truth. What is that special sound the truth has?

I can feel the tension at the table. There is an electricity that flows from Andy to Chuck to Senna and on to me.

I go on. "I wasn't into that scene," I say. "Coke isn't my drug of choice. I only know what Hannah told me about it." I want them to understand that even what I know might not be the truth, but if it isn't, these aren't my lies—they're Hannah's lies. So far, I've said nothing about any of the guys, but they all watch me, silently. Senna is no doubt an enemy. I've given a name. I've given the cops something to go on.

The adults look shocked and suspicious. My heart misses a beat and I try to think fast. I should not have said anything right here in front of all of them, but it's too late.

Elise widens her swollen eyes, and makes a small croaking sound. I glance at her but it's too painful and I have to look away. Elise's face is the face of someone whose life as she knew it is over. It's the face of someone whose mind is playing a tape, a simple loop, in which all they can think is *No*.

My mom, I can tell, is asking herself what the hell will I say next.

Alan Scott finally breaks the silence. His voice is rough and deep. "So Marcelle, you knew Hannah was in trouble with these people, this drug dealer, and you didn't say anything about this until now?" He looks around the table, disbelieving. I am one of those terrible people, like the Germans during the Holocaust, who knows everything and does nothing. Mom starts to speak, and so do both of Hannah's parents. That's when the detective stands and holds up his hand.

"Dr. Henry, I think the young lady and her mother should take a break at this point?" There's crying coming from some-where. I think it's Elise, but maybe Alan, too, and then I start—hot tears run down my cheeks. I bawl too hard to speak, although a part of me wants to say so much more.

I don't remember leaving the room, but suddenly we are outside in the sunshine. The clouds that seemed to be gathering have blown away, and the wind has calmed.

Mom walks next to me, and occasionally pats my back, her touch light and indecisive, like she can't quite commit to comforting me. The detective meets us on the walkway in front of the glass side doors no one ever uses. He puts his hand on my shoulder and peers at me with his light eyes, the lashes surprisingly long and thickly blond at the edges. I can't remember his name, and since he's plainclothes there's no tag. Was it Pedro? Pablo?

"You did good in there, kid, you hear? You did good." He nods sharply at me, then at Mom. I'm crying too hard to say anything. I feel grateful to the detective. At least he seems like he's doing something, like he's in his element and not, like everyone else, too stunned to think. He thinks I did good. *He knows what it means in this situation to be good*, I tell myself.

Then the detective turns to my mom, "Take care of her. We'll line something up for an interview? I can come by the house and interview her. No patrol car. No uniforms. Just me." My mom nods. I know there is something terrible in these words, something I still can't get my brain to take in. *He's a cop. A real cop, and he wants to talk to me about Hannah.*

"I don't believe my daughter knows much more than she has stated, but I will have an attorney present at any meeting.

I'll call with times." My mom is sticking it to the guy, and I feel unnerved by this. I want to talk to him and no one else, not some lawyer who will confuse me. I want to tell the truth. I want to help—help Hannah.

But then again I know Mom is right and there are other people involved, not only me. There's Jonas, and there's Andy. Everyone I'm friends with had something to do with Hannah's deal with Alex.

"As you wish," he says. "If it were my kid, I'd do the same." The detective is maybe late thirties, early forties. I wonder for an instant about his kids. Are they good, or were they like me? Probably too young to tell.

Mom and I walk together to our car. There's not even any question of my going to class, even though this means missing math, and I usually freak if I have to miss math. I can bear not being supersmart, but I can't bear dropping AP math. It's bad enough being Rehab Girl. I need something in my life to be okay, and school has always been this for me—proof that I'm not a total piece of shit.

I let out a cough-like sob, and Mom grabs my shoulder. I try to pull myself together, to stop being a spectacle.

I climb into the car and fold myself in half, with my face in my hands. I picture Mr. Hellman, my math teacher, asking the class where I am, and people exchanging glances and saying nothing.

Silently, Mom starts driving.

I'm afraid to talk to Andy and afraid not to. I feel for my phone in my pocket. I want to text Andy to meet me at Michiko's tonight, but who knows if my parents will let me out of the house. I don't know if my parents will even let me go to the Center, or if I'll be under some sort of house arrest, on lockdown, for knowing just enough to scare half the town shitless.

I have no idea what Senna will do now that I have outed him to the cops. I'm a snitch. Maybe most people who rat out their friends feel like they have no choice; they have to rat, or they'll be blamed themselves. Or maybe they're like me, and something inside them has broken free—like one of those old-fashioned wind-up toys, where you turn the handle until, finally, something pops out on a spring—an animal head or a clown. I've been holding something inside myself since that night we went to Alex's, and he shut the door behind him—since he trapped me and touched me.

Maybe he thought I was like Hannah. I could never stop Hannah from doing whatever she wanted. I still don't know where she is, or if she's coming back. But I did something today I never expected to do—I stopped Alex. I still feel shaky from that moment when I said his name. I know I shocked everyone. I know nobody thought I had it in me.

Mom drives slowly down our street. People have their Halloween decorations up, but for a minute I can't remember whether Halloween has passed or not. I feel a tightness in my stomach as we pull in our driveway. What if it's really true— that something terrible has happened, and that this isn't some

Hannah stunt—some craziness she's pulled everyone into?

People are saying Hannah Scott is *missing*. But *missing* is not a terrible-sounding word. I think of how a glove is missing, or a piece of some thousand-piece puzzle. *Missing* is for things that you can replace, or that hardly matter in the first place.

I miss Hannah. But I missed her before she disappeared, too. There was always something missing. Maybe that's why she could stand there in front of the camera, in front of strangers, and feel like nothing was real.

TWENTY-TWO

MY LAWYER'S NAME is Barbara Fine. I meet with her tomorrow after I go to the Center. Detective Perez will come here as well. I hear Mom in the kitchen tell Perez, "Listen, she doesn't know where she was or who she was with. I know what's at stake, believe me," but in the end it sounds like he agrees on tomorrow. If I knew something that would give the cops more to go on, a way to focus their search, I'd talk to Mom. I'd call Perez myself. But I don't. I said enough in the meeting at school for the cops to get the details when they talk to Senna, Chuck, and Jonas. Senna and Jonas are the people who know exactly what Alex was doing with Hannah. They know his last name, his address, where he's from.

From the couch in the den, I listen as Mom makes more calls—to Dad, and to Barbara Fine. I fold my arms over my face and shut my eyes. I'm both jittery and weirdly exhausted—on the verge of slipping into a restless sleep, so that what Mom is saying in the other room seems both real and the product of some dimly recalled nightmare.

I suppose by now the cops are searching every inch of Playland Park, of the nature preserve, the marshland filled with cattails and skunk cabbage, dog shit and weird, skittish animals—beavers, muskrats, swamp-smelling rodents that give you a heart attack when they pop out of the tall, dense reeds. Dad and I used to go to the preserve for walks when I was little. He liked to smoke an occasional cigar, which Mom hated and refused to be around. I always thought the smell was kind of nice, sweet and musky. I liked the way Dad would stop to name all the birds he saw, sandpipers, herons, egrets, and ibises. I was proud he could tell one bird from the other by their shape or the color of their legs.

When it's quiet in the kitchen, I force myself to get up and talk to Mom. I climb on one of the kitchen stools and watch as she takes out a package of chicken, puts it in a bowl in the sink, and turns on the water. She doesn't look at me until I speak.

"So, that's all set?" I ask. "Am I going to school tomorrow? What about the Center?" Mom picks up a dish towel and wipes her hands. For a moment, she looks angry, and then you can see she's counting to ten or something, trying to control herself, because her voice is annoyingly neutral and flat. "Yes, Marcelle, you'll go back to school tomorrow. As for the Center, that's even more critical. I can't understand how you could even question your need for support at this point."

I feel like she's not understanding me on purpose. "No, I

mean, of course I'll go back, but just for now. I'm really tired, and we don't know how long everything will take, and I have all this work, and there's Michiko's . . ." I trail off because Michiko's is overstepping, I know. But going to Michiko's will be my only chance to talk to Andy, and to find out what's happening with Jonas. I want to know if what I said at the meeting will clue people in to Jonas's part in things. I want Jonas to speak up, but I want to know Andy is okay—that the cops will leave him out of it, and that his parents will see that it was Jonas, not Andy, who got everybody so fucked up. Andy brought Jonas around to Senna's, but he did what anyone would do. He just put people in touch who wanted the same thing. Maybe that's a lame defense. I know it is. But Andy isn't bad. I know that, too. It's not like he could somehow see the future.

Mom puts her hands on her hips and says, "You need to meet all of your obligations, Marcelle. Not only when it's comfortable, but each and every day, just like your dad and me. I know you did your best today, but unfortunately, you chose to be honest too late in the game. I don't blame you for Hannah's actions, not at all. You can't take that on yourself. But you do need to think about what you've done and what you have failed to do. You're upset right now, we all are, but what you need to do going forward is stay on your own path and not get distracted and make excuses because of the risks other people are taking."

I nod and look serious, as though going to Michiko's was something I dreaded.

I think about the homework I have to get done, and how I have to spend two hours at the Center this afternoon, somehow convincing the group that I should be there. I don't know how I can focus on any of it with Hannah out there—with Hannah *gone.*

TWENTY-THREE

UPSTAIRS, AT MY desk, I try to teach myself today's Precalculus lesson off the classroom website, but I've visited five pages and am still confused. I look at the homework and sigh. I can't do it, not even the first, and likely the easiest, of the ten problems. I decide I'm better off starting with Center work, especially since I have to go get stared down by the group in an hour. If my mom knew what things were really like in Group, I think she'd let me take a break. After the meeting at school today, I can hardly get my head around having to sit through another ninety-minute torture session.

I take out the yellow pad where I started writing with Kevin yesterday. My accountability letter is supposed to say clearly and without excuses the things I did that got me into trouble, that landed me under Michiko's parked car, and then in the emergency room with my blood alcohol level so high the doctor wondered why I was still breathing. I chew on my pen. How do

I draw the line between my shit and everybody else's?

I didn't tell Hannah to stop. I didn't tell Hannah she was going too far. I spoke up, but only once it was too late. When Hannah showed me the other stuff she bought, not the clothes, but the sex shop toys, I sat down on the bed and picked up each one. They were still wrapped in plastic and had names like "The Rabbit" and "The Suregasm." At first glance, they looked like baby toys.

"You bought all this stuff?" I asked. She grinned and nodded. "In the city. It was hilarious," she said. "The girls in the store are really professional. No one acts like there's anything wrong or pervy about it." Hannah looked down at the crap on the bed, and then suddenly gathered it up and stuck it back in the box.

"Don't look at me like that, Marce," she said. "It's not like you're some fucking saint." With the black wig, Hannah's eyes looked amber. Her cheekbones were more prominent. She was so thin, so frail. But none of that made her beautiful. It was something else—a quality that isn't really physical.

Maybe it's that she's freer than other people. Or more trapped. Braver. Or more afraid. Whatever it is, I was in awe of her one minute, and in the next instant, I wanted to shake her. I guess a part of me always wanted to *be* her. Whatever her magical quality was, I wanted to have it too. I can't tell now if I'm even over that—or if she came back tonight I'd feel exactly the same way.

Hannah chased the light that coke gave her—the brilliant

light. She chased the darkness Alex showed her—the darkness that makes a person something to buy or sell.

I take out my iPad and I write about everything I did that led to my crash on the Death Wish night. I write about loving beer and vodka. I write about riding my bike away from Andy, cutting through the woods in the dark between our neighborhood and Senna's. About Andy and me shit-faced in Senna's garage, banging into the lawn mower, the snow shovels, the ladder, cans of paint; of being dirty, bruised, hungover, and fucked up out of my brain.

I curl up on my bed with my pink-fringed throw blanket that covers everything but my feet.

My toes are cold. I feel sick.

Hannah's phone has been found with more than one set of fingerprints. . . . That sentence has poisoned me.

I picture the phone in its sparkly gold-toned case lying in the mud in the reeds and swampy mess behind Playland. I try to force my brain to think about Hannah herself, but all I can see in my mind is the dark and the dirt.

TWENTY-FOUR

AT 3:20 IT'S almost time for Mom to take me to the Center. She says she'll bring me to Michiko's after, but that she'll wait in her car for me there while I take care of the bird and Marco. That means no meeting Andy. I need to hear what he has to say about the meeting at school, about Hannah's phone and the two sets of fingerprints. Mostly I need to hear his voice, and to know what's happening between us is still real.

Dad gets home a few minutes before Mom and I are supposed to leave. He puts down his briefcase, which is one of those black vinyl types, nothing fancy. He stands by the door in his corduroys and tweed jacket, his usual non-meeting work clothes.

He puts his hand on my shoulder as I head toward the door. I'm tall enough to look him right in the eye. "We're going to the Center," I say. "I've got Group."

"I'd like to come," Dad says.

"Come?" I ask. "But it's Group. It's led by other kids. I don't have any other meetings scheduled."

"I want to get a feel for this place, see what it's doing for you," Dad says. I try to get my head around this. Dad came to the hospital the night of my accident; he was there when they pumped my stomach, but other than that he's let Mom handle "the situation." I get the feeling he's rethinking things, believing there must be more he can do. We've talked about this sort of thing in Group—how parents try to rescue you, once they realize things have gotten serious. But it's almost always by doing something useless, like what Dad is doing now.

I don't know why Dad thinks if he tags along anything will be different. Hannah is missing. He can't change that.

But that's not what I say to Dad. Instead, I take a deep breath and say what no one has said all day, but that everyone's been thinking. "Dad," I ask in a husky, strange-sounding voice, "do you think that Hannah is dead?"

He stares at me. "I think most of us are wondering that same thing, honey. Actually, a lot of people are wondering what *you* think." He speaks in a near-whisper. I nod.

If I could get my head to stop aching for more than a minute, or if I could talk things out with Andy, I might be able to snap the pieces together of this broken chain. But without Andy, with just my own throbbing brain, I can't get anywhere.

I walk out the kitchen door toward Mom's car, stuck between Mom and Dad. I sit in the back of the car like a little kid.

The world goes by in a blur. I stare out the window. I don't feel sorry only for myself, but for everything and everyone we pass. Everything seems stuck being a part of something else that's being ruined by roads, cars, trash, people. I don't know how much being sober matters. But then again, being a fuck-up in a fucked-up world hasn't worked out too well, either.

It has been almost three days since I've heard from Hannah, depending on how you count Sunday. At one point in the car, when we're stopped at a light, I think I see her. But it's some other small dark-haired girl on her bike, waiting for the light to change. When she turns her head, I see she has a little button nose and full, rosy cheeks—none of Hannah's strange beauty, the high cheekbones, full lips, eyes that say yes, no, everything, all the time. No, not Hannah, just a regular girl.

Mom decides not to come into the Center. She says she'll wait in the car. She takes out her phone, and barely looks up when Dad and I get out and walk toward the building. Outside, it's warm and hazy. The streetlamps cast a strange light, and somehow as we walk toward the Center the building looks blurry, like it's fading into the sky, and like it doesn't really exist as brick and glass.

Some rich ex-drunk left his money to the Center for New Living, and this is where they put it, one block over from the strip mall, right across from Citibank, three blocks from the police station. Only no one ever mentions the Center, even though they drive right past it practically every day.

Inside, I nod to the security guy who leans on his desk, eating an apple. He knows my face, and doesn't question either me or Dad. Once you're a Center kid, you can come and go as you please.

I can see Dad taking it all in. He looks confused, even embarrassed. I can tell none of it is what he expected, no antiseptic hospital smell, no busy receptionist putting callers on hold. It's about half as official-feeling as the town library.

Kevin's door is shut tight, and a small African-American woman sits alone on the couch in the barren waiting area. She could be Martin's mom, or who knows, maybe a new kid is starting. I can see James through the open doorway in the Group room, notebook in front of him. He wears his usual button-down. His hair looks freshly cut. Cyndi is in the little kitchenette wearing sheepskin slippers and sweatpants. She keeps her slippers in the cubbies, where everyone is supposed to leave their school stuff. It's like she wants everyone to know how at home she is here.

I peer into the Group room, and I see Martin is there too, bent over the far end of the table, writing on a yellow pad. He wears headphones and rocks to the beat of his music. This is allowed until Group actually begins.

I tell Dad Group is starting, and he takes a seat on the couch outside Kevin's office. "You're waiting?" I ask. Dad picks up a pamphlet from the coffee table. I'm afraid Dad thinks he can walk right into Group, or burst into Kevin's office. You aren't allowed to do stuff like that at the Center. I want to explain that, while it seems laid-back, there are all kinds of rules, invisible rules you have to learn by breaking them.

Dad stares at me. He has an unfamiliar, scared-animal look to him, but he speaks in his usual Dad-the-rational-scientist voice. "Your mom and I think you need some support right now, and maybe . . ." He trails off. ". . . some protection." For the first time it occurs to me that Dad might not be furious at me, or even suspicious. My father is afraid. It suddenly makes sense. They think it's possible that whatever happened to Hannah could happen to me.

TWENTY-FIVE

I CATCH JAMES'S eye as he peers out of the Group room, nod, and pick up my book bag, leaving Dad on the couch with the Center pamphlet unopened on his lap. Just as I pass, Kevin's door opens, and I hear voices. Out of the corner of my eye, I glimpse a familiar woman—tall and slender, with hair down to her chin in a neat bob. She's all polish and gloss. Then I recognize a voice. And there, at the Center, coming forward to greet me with a shy smile, is Chuck.

"Marcelle," Kevin says. "On your way to Group?" I nod, mute. "I think you may know Chuck Glasser?" I nod again. "Chuck is considering joining us. You two have outside contact?"

"We hang out with the same group," I say. "I mean, social group."

"Understood," Kevin says. "Well, we have a special way of handling this sort of thing."

We are all standing in the hallway, Chuck, his mom, Kevin, and me. Dad is down the hall, and I can't tell if he can hear what's going down, but Kevin catches me looking his way.

"Dad?" Kevin asks. I nod again, and Kevin slow-jogs over to where Dad is, and they do the quick handshake and then Kevin calls us all back over to the waiting area.

"Here's our deal," Kevin starts again, pulling nervously at his beard. "We are a peer-based program, and we run on the honor system. Kids support kids. Therapists are here to get kids ready to be Group members, to work out goals, and to get kids started on being accountable. Once a kid gets what accountability really means to the Group, the kids basically run the show and old folks like me oversee the process. Group leaders are trained to take detailed minutes of each meeting. I read the minutes every morning. I can tell you the kids have a fantastic handle on what makes other kids tick. It's pretty brilliant."

Kevin pauses and glances at Mrs. Glasser and my dad, who nod as if they immediately get what Kevin is saying, which I can tell they don't. "You two, Marcelle and Chuck, are what's considered an OC pair. Meaning you two have outside contact. There are three rules for OCs. He holds up two fingers: One, no discussing the Group outside of Group time. Two, no bringing in outside shit. You, Marcelle, do not bring Chuck's outside stuff in. Vice versa. One exception is if you, Chuck, or you, Marcelle, see the other engage in substance abuse. Not hear about it, but see it, got it?" We both nod. "Third thing: You're both out on your asses if either of you violate the other two rules."

I start to drift and can't really focus on what Kevin is saying. Chuck is here, at the Center. It feels like an eternity ago that he told me he was thinking about giving up blow. But this? Something is wrong. What exactly is "outside shit"? I have no idea what to say, so I keep silent. My throat feels parched and the feverish feeling returns.

Dad breaks in suddenly. "How is that fair?" he asks. "If Chuck violates the rules, why would Marcelle be asked to leave? Why is her membership in jeopardy?"

"Ah," Kevin says. "Great question, Dad. It's about mutual trust. If Marcelle can't trust the group, she can't support the group either. She'd have to reapply even if Chuck violates her. So, as OCs, they really are partners, and need to sign the OC contract. Here's the other thing. You, Marcelle, have been accepted as a probationary Group member. As far as we know, you've surpassed your 'cold two,' or so you say. You started on some goals. You've been introduced to the accountability structure—the accountability narrative or letter or whatever the fuck you guys call that thing is complete or will be by end of today. So, you have until tomorrow's Group to decide whether you can trust Chuck. If you say no, no questions asked, Chuck is out. If you say, yes, the two of you are bound together. You succeed or fail only if you both abide by the confidentiality structure. Got it? You have a day to decide."

Dad stares at Kevin, his mouth slightly open. I can tell he's starting to get the picture about the Center, that it's not just talking about your problems or reading about teen issues like you do in health class at school. It's an after-school bizarro universe. It's emotional purgatory. It's peer pressure turned on its head, supposedly for our own good. It's bullying each other into sobriety. It's totally fucked.

Now, here is beautiful blue-eyed Chuck, and I have to decide, in twenty-four hours, where we stand. There is no way Kevin, or Dad, can understand what a huge question that is.

"So, Marcelle, okay if Chuck joins as a silent participant today, gets a feel for Group? You can take a pass on Feedback today if doing Feedback in front of Chuck makes you uncomfortable before you've made up your mind."

I look at Dad, and he nods, as though he sees how all of this makes sense. But I wonder if in the real world the Center makes any sense at all. I can't decide whether Chuck coming to the Center is a good sign—a sign that he, too, is out of his depth, scared of what's gone down, or if I'm not being paranoid in thinking Chuck is here because he and Senna think I know more than I do about where Hannah is, and about what may have happened to her. I've half sold everybody out. But what that really means now that Hannah is missing, I haven't a clue.

"Welcome to therapy land," I say to Chuck. "Say goodbye to your old brain."

TWENTY-SIX

CHUCK LETS ME go in first, pauses in the kitchenette, and gets himself a Coke. Then he takes a seat directly across the table from me. He opens the Coke, takes a sip, and looks around, appearing perfectly within his element watching the other kids file into Group, as though this were his hundredth day here and not his first. Chuck has two speeds, I think. There's this calm, cool Chuck, and there's the Chuck that Senna brings out—wild, flailing Chuck.

I sit between James and Cyndi, a seat away from Ali. Martin is at the opposite side of the table, next to Chuck, with Maria at the end on Chuck's other side. Martin turns to shake Chuck's hand and this leads James to call us to order. We get introduced to newbies by the book.

"So we'll start today's meeting by introducing Chuck, a new prospective member of our Group," James says. "Um, Chuck, usually we have new prospectives give a little intro and fully participate, but since you and Marcelle are OCs, we really have to hold out on participation until tomorrow, when Marcelle can address whether she feels comfortable with you here. Okay? We can't have new members throw the balance off, and you know Marcelle has skin in the game."

At the Center everyone talks about *skin in the game*, which is basically to say you've done your cold two, have Goals, are becoming accountable, and you've shown up at a bunch of meetings. If you fuck up at the Center, like get high or drunk, you can come back, reapply, and if you have enough "skin-in," they'll let you return, even if you slip up or relapse. "Skin-in" can keep you from getting bounced, as long as you're making a real attempt to live substance-free. Other stuff will get you kicked out right away, like hitting on someone, violating confidentiality, or trash-talking anyone. Any kind of hostility or aggression at all will get you booted. James saying I have *skin-in* isn't like him saying they all *like* me and want me to be here, it's just a standard membership rule.

I watch how Chuck reacts to James, which is basically saying I'm watching for Chuck to reveal nothing at all of his innermost thoughts or feelings. I've been in classes with Chuck at school. He never goofs off or zones out. He isn't like other people that way. He's just there, embodying Chuckness. His mind must be more spongelike than other people's because he never seems to be working all that hard, but unlike me, he stays in honors classes seemingly without effort.

James scans the room, then opens the floor to everyone

to speak, and Ali, looking hyped and jittery, gets the session rolling.

Ali starts about how he is tired of his parents not trusting him, and it's hard, he says, to trust himself, when everyone is always looking at him like he's going to burn the house down, which he almost did when he was obsessively gaming in his basement and let a candle burn down to the wooden table. The only thing that saved him was that his sister had cut last period gym. When she got home, she smelled smoke and found the smoldering candle melting into the tabletop and Ali, stoned and using the candle to hide the smell, glued to his PlayStation. If she'd stayed the whole day at school, Ali wouldn't be here whining about her and the rest of his family.

Chuck appears to be listening closely to Ali, drinking his Coke, narrowing his piercing gaze. "I've been clean four months," Ali says. "I mean, I was a game junkie and a pothead, okay, got that. But I'm almost eighteen and I have a *curfew*. My dad is still so pissed at the sight of me, I don't know, it makes me want to punch him in the face. He pays the fucking bills all right, but then the rest of the time he's on his ass, reading his fucking newspaper and making my mom and sister wait on him. I'm embarrassed for them, you know? The way he acts like he's a god and they exist to serve him."

Ali pauses and takes a deep breath. He has tears in his eyes, and I feel sorry for him, but his last Group session started off this way too, with Ali spewing shit about hating his father, complaining about his own depression, laziness, and procrastination.

I begin to wonder what's the point. I look around and James, Cyndi, and Martin all look bored.

"Jesus," Ali finally says, winding down. "I just don't know how long I can take living with the fat slob." I bristle a little at this, especially since no one calls Ali on his anti-fat thing. If he said something blatantly racist or sexist, the group would shut him down.

I try to think about what Ali is saying, but my head is spinning and my stomach lurches. Tomorrow I meet with Barbara Fine. Detective Perez will come over too. I need to tell him what I know. But first I have to understand it for myself, which is hard without Hannah to talk to. I wish I knew either more or less than I do. What I know is a sketch of a story, but not the story itself.

I try to go back to Sunday night in my mind, when I got the text from Hannah asking me to lie. Why did she go dark immediately after? Who was she with over there in the Marshlands?

I can take a pass at Group today because of Chuck being here, but I have my Goals I need to work on and I have my accountability letter I need to get feedback on and polish up.

There was plenty to tell in my letter that didn't involve Hannah. There was the beer and vodka I drank in my room. There were those blurry, boozy nights at Senna's. But mostly there was the belief I had, and I guess still have, that getting through the day without alcohol is too hard. Time always moves too fast or too slow. There's always something I want to skip over or forget. Even if everything is great, I want more, or I want less. I don't know if this makes me an addict or not. Maybe, when things calm down, I can ask the others what they think. Today, I don't know what will come out of my mouth.

I twitch in my seat, waiting for Ali's feedback to end, but everyone has something to say. Ali is weepy, and Martin gives him a tissue and pats him on the back.

"I hear you, man," Martin says. You aren't supposed to talk about yourself during someone else's Group, so Martin doesn't say exactly what he means, but we all know Martin's parents still hardly let him go out. Martin was caught dealing Percocet at his fancy private school across the county. He ended up with a suspension. His partner in crime was a white kid whose parents thought Martin was a bad influence. Turns out it was their kid with the connections. Martin says he never ratted.

Ali blows his nose and leans back in his chair. "That's it," he says. "Maybe I just live like this until college. Another year and a half under house arrest."

James looks around the table. "That's it? Anyone want to wrap it up?"

I raise my hand. I suddenly feel compelled to say something, maybe just to prove to Chuck that I actually belong here.

"Maybe you can earn trust by letting your parents see you go somewhere with a friend? With someone who's sober?" I see heads nod around the table.

"I'd do that with you, man," Martin says. "We could toss a ball around at Flint, or go for a run. Maybe our dads could talk." Ali nods vigorously. I feel bad for the guy. I know how it feels.

The cage is closing in on me, too.

Feeling good that my suggestion for Ali got some traction, I raise three fingers, the sign for wanting the Group's attention. Three fingers, I read in the pamphlet last night, is to remind us that Group time is for focused discussion on our three big goals.

I note the way Chuck seemingly involuntarily ducks his head when James calls on me. I wish I knew what he was thinking.

"I'm addressing my accountability," I hear myself say, "which I think includes all my Goals?" James nods. I'm doing it right for once. I'm supposed to bring all of my questions and struggles to the Group, but you can't just say whatever comes into your head here; it's all according to rules and procedures I don't yet understand, and maybe never will.

"I have some questions about what I'm writing," I say. "I'm not sure where my accountability is." Everyone perks up at this, and I can feel my heart skip a beat. I think I see Martin and Ali exchange glances, looks that say something like *What the hell is this girl getting herself into?*

James holds up his hand for me to stop. In any other context this would be rude, but he's James, Prince of the Fuck-ups.

"Wow, Marcelle, that's not where I thought you were going." He pauses for effect, although everyone is already alert, anticipating the show to come. "Anyone?" he asks, scanning the table for volunteers to chew me up and spit me out, once again. "I thought for sure you were already on this, Marcelle. Maybe I'm wrong about how much skin you have in?" He looks right at Chuck when he says this.

I see Chuck sit up straighter. I'm not sure exactly what's

happening, but I fear I'm about to be demoted from prospective member to non-member for that one statement. I'm supposed to ask for help here, but I'm not supposed to actually need it.

Cyndi looks even more impatient than usual. "Marcelle, accountability has to be exactly that. *Where is your account-ability?* That's not a concept. We don't *locate* blame outside ourselves. You need to be fully prepared to enact your Goals wherever you are, whatever other people are doing. We aren't about our influences here. We are about our potential. Asking where your accountability is, that's like rejecting this Group and everything we stand for. You need to use us for support. But we aren't your mirror. Whoever else you are thinking about within your accountability narrative, they aren't your mirror, either. It sounds like you're still in the Funhouse."

Everyone nods, and Martin even gives a short, curt laugh. Chuck stares hard at Cyndi. I don't know why he doesn't look more confused.

I know what the Funhouse is. Last week, Cyndi had Group on her Funhouse. It has something to do with not seeing other people for who they are, and just seeing how they see you, and your distortions of them. Like you see people as disgusting or frightening, not because this is what they *are*, but it's how your feelings make them seem. Cyndi talked a lot about her father, how she thinks her father sees her as a whore and she sees him as evil incarnate.

I sigh deeply. There is nothing to do but stop trying to speak this foreign language, and to say what I actually have to say.

"I'm not sure," I start again. "I know I'm accountable for my drinking and the other stuff I was doing—smoking weed, not saying where I was, the accident, getting hurt, scaring my parents."

The mood in the group shifts, and I can feel even Cyndi urging me on, but they are making me nervous, hanging on my words, listening too close. Chuck leans back in his chair; his eyes are closed and he folds his hands on the table. Somewhere in all this mess is a way out. I want my way out to be the way to find Hannah. But I won't know anything more, won't be any closer to helping find her, until I begin the story again. Somehow, I think if I can get the story exactly right, a clue will fall into place. I'll know why Chuck is here. I'll be strong enough to go on.

"But drinking wasn't my only shit," I continue. "I also used people." I know I am on the right track. Everyone watches me now, waiting to hear what I have to say. "I'm going to say that Chuck, my OC, was someone I used. I used to try to see other people, and myself, through his eyes. This wasn't good for me. It was a way of putting myself down all the time. I think Chuck is superior to me somehow, or smarter than me."

Chuck opens his eyes and stares at me. He is pale, his dark blue eyes glittery, impossible to read. Chuck only opens up when Senna or Hannah are around. I can't recall him ever even smiling directly at me, or laughing at anything I've said. Why, I wonder, have I ever thought of him as a friend at all?

My heart beats so hard and so fast I feel like my chest must be visibly shaking. My voice is otherworldly, an echo coming from deep inside me. I'm nauseous, but I also feel weirdly hollow, almost hungry. There is an emptiness inside me that threatens to swallow me. I'm a human black hole.

"My biggest fuck-up is with Hannah," I continue. "I didn't help her. I didn't help her because I was afraid of her. And Senna, and Chuck, and maybe even Andy a little, too. When I realized something bad might be happening, I didn't tell anyone the things I knew Hannah was doing." I stop and look blindly around the table. "I'm still keeping some of Hannah's secrets. I can't tell if I'm protecting her or myself."

There is dead silence in the room. Then Ali, in his soft, singsongy voice, says the word I realize I'm waiting for: *"Why?"*

"I think Hannah might be dead," I say bluntly. "They found her phone in a park. The nature preserve near Playland. They say there are two sets of fingerprints on it." I can tell everyone has made the connection now between me and the missing girl they heard about over the course of the day. Our school sent out a mass email. No doubt the neighboring towns have done the same.

I take a deep breath and dive in again. "I wish I had called someone when Hannah texted me before she disappeared. I should have told my mother that she had asked me to lie for her. But I was still seeing Hannah as someone whose voice mattered more than mine. Hannah mattered more than me. Hannah was my mirror."

James nods quickly, leaning forward, concentrating entirely

on me. "Are you saying, Marcelle, if you hadn't seen Hannah as someone above you, better than you, you might have asked her more questions, or told her mom right away that she was lying?"

"Maybe," I say. "I loved being *around* Hannah. But I don't know if I love—or loved—Hannah." Everyone is silent. Chuck stands up, walks slowly around the large wooden table to the garbage can by the door, and tosses his Coke can in it noisily. He doesn't look at anyone. I wonder at Chuck's timing. I can't help but feel if it were someone else, James might have raised his eyebrows, or Cyndi might have commented on how we don't usually get up during someone's Group.

It occurs to me in that moment that even James and Cyndi might succumb to Chuck's weird, silent power, that Group, with all its expectations and special words for things, might not really be any different from the real world after all. Even as they drill me about my so-called Funhouse, about Hannah's power over me, Chuck is gaining ground within the Group itself. Maybe, I think, there is no such thing as a place to escape to, to get away from other people's shit, or even your own shit. Maybe places like the Center are Funhouses, too, places where you think you know people, but really who they are is all tangled up with your own ideas about yourself.

Maybe I'm alone, even here.

James snaps his fingers and brings me out of my thoughts. When the Group leader snaps, it means the Group is acknowledging that you're working at a goal, or a step in the program, like accountability. "I hear you taking accountability, Marcelle, for keeping Hannah's secrets. But not for her doing dangerous things. I think maybe you are moving away from putting Hannah on a pedestal. I think you get the idea that you can't blame Hannah for your problems no matter how big Hannah's problems are."

I nod.

I feel Chuck's eyes on me from across the table. I glance up and meet his gaze, meet that impenetrable Chuck Glasser stare.

TWENTY-SEVEN

WHEN WE ALL come out of Group, Dad is still there on the couch, only he's put down the Center pamphlet and his eyes are closed. I had forgotten about him being my bodyguard.

James stands with me while Dad collects himself and wipes nap-drool from the corner of his mouth with his shirtsleeve. "Good work in there, Marcelle," James says. I half smile.

"Thanks," I say. For a second, James seems like a regular kid, a semi-cute guy with bad skin and an awkward smile.

Dad nods to James and shakes his hand.

"Have a good evening," Dad says. James says nothing, but pats me on the back as I walk away. I hate myself for how good it feels to have James's approval.

Dad and I drive along in silence until we hit the light at Broadway. Dad drove Mom home right after Group started, so he didn't actually stay at the Center guarding me the whole time, which makes my family seem marginally less crazy.

Dad clears his throat. "Seems intense in there," he says. "Not exactly warm and fuzzy." Dad has bags under his eyes and seems to be having trouble staying focused on the road. He keeps glancing my way, as though I am about to sprout a second head.

"I don't think you and Mom really did a lot of research before getting me in there," I say. I know this is true. They were freaking out about my accident. They just went with what Dr. Hagan said was best. I'm about to start explaining how weird it is that Chuck is at the Center, when I realize Dad is going right home and forgetting all about Michiko's. When I remind him, he stays silent, but makes a right onto Summit.

"I won't be long, okay?" I say as I bolt out of the car.

"You know you're on a short leash these days, kid," Dad says as I shut the heavy door to the SUV. I don't say anything to Dad, but nod so he knows I hear him and that I'm not fighting with him.

The house feels eerily empty. Even the bird is quiet for once. In the kitchen, I switch on the lights and open the usual tuna. In seconds, Marco races in on nearly silent paws and leaps up on the counter, so I have to push him off to get the can fully opened. He jumps right back up and I open the can with Marco's head cradled in my elbow.

When I'm through with the cat, I pull the birdseed from the lower kitchen cabinet, beneath Michiko's glistening bar. There's a tall, narrow bottle of vodka, a square, clear bottle of gin, a bottle of vermouth, and another bright green liquor that looks like cough medicine. None of her stuff is brands I've heard of. It's all organic and small batch. Above the bar are her wine, highball, and martini glasses, all spotlessly clean. To the right are three unopened bottles of red wine, the labels in French. Somehow, all of these things seem to me to be for show, as if Michiko were waiting for some James Bond–like guy to strut into her immaculate suburban living room so she could make him the perfect drink.

I wonder what I would do if any of these bottles were open— would I sneak a shot? With Dad outside waiting, I wouldn't. But if he weren't there, and my life was more or less back to normal, I might. If Hannah showed up at school in the morning and, just like that, everything went back to normal, why wouldn't I sneak a bit now and then? Who says I couldn't learn to drink like everybody else? Do people expect me and the rest of the Center kids to live sober for the rest of our lives, just because when we were young, we fucked up and got caught?

I pour the birdseed into the empty white dish as Bird dances from one foot to the other in what I suppose is excitement. A good friend would have done something. A real friend would have been sick at the sight of Hannah in that long black wig.

I'm about to shut the birdcage when I hear a tapping on the glass door behind me. I nearly scream, even though a part of me knows without question it's Andy. It's what I wanted, and half expected, but I'm still scared out of my mind by the shock.

I open the door, my heart still beating so hard, it's difficult to talk. Andy leans against the door, not coming all the way in. I can smell his lemon-scented soap. I can see his dark spiky hair silhouetted against the outside light. He must have ridden his bike to the side of the house, and cut through the lawn, away from where my dad waits in the driveway.

"Jesus Christ," I say. "Are you trying to get me grounded for eternity?" I ask.

"Sorry," Andy whispers, his lips almost touching mine. His eyes look tight with fear. "I wanted to make sure you were okay," he says.

I shake my head no, blinking back tears. "What about you?" I ask.

"The cops called." Andy ducks his head. I wonder if he's crying. "I don't know where Jonas is. Not answering his phone. The cops were calling for him." We're holding hands now. I don't know how this has happened, whether I reached for his or he reached for mine. His palms are soft and dry. On impulse, I pull him close in one of those hugs that you don't know how to end once they start.

Where could Jonas be? Far away if he had any brains, or money.

"He's my brother, Marci," Andy mumbles in my ear. "If we don't say anything, maybe no one will know he was . . ." He doesn't finish, as though even in a whisper it's too messed up to say the words.

I want to blame someone for everything that's happening. Jonas is a loser. If he'd only gone away to school, no one would ever have met Alex. There'd barely be any coke. We'd have partied the way we always had.

Then there's Senna. None of this could have happened without him. Senna was the one who wanted to get a stash and deal.

There's Hannah herself. How much of this was Hannah's own fault? I get a chill thinking about it.

"Does anyone even care what happened to her?" I say this in Andy's ear, not so much to him, but to myself.

Andy sniffles. "I care," he mumbles into my hair. I want him to be brave, to have a plan. But I know this is hopeless. What's happened to Hannah, whatever it is, is a disaster for him and for his parents, as well as the Scotts. I get a giant lump in my throat. Andy has to rat out Jonas. We both know this.

We hold each other in Michiko's kitchen. I know I've been gone too long, but I don't let go of Andy and he doesn't let go of me, either.

"I've gotta go, Andy," I whisper finally. "My dad will murder me if he sees you here."

"I know," Andy says. Then he kisses me—a deep kiss, a movie kiss. We are that I-don't-know-when-I'll-see-you-again couple.

I shut and lock Michiko's front door. Michiko's white rose bushes still bloom alongside the driveway, where I nearly died.

Dad has left the lights on and the engine running. I wonder how long I've been inside. He's looking at his phone, his hair rumpled, his mouth pulled tight in concentration.

When I get in the car, he's about to say something, but

then stops and stares at the dashboard. He has the radio on. In the next second my head begins to throb. It's like thunder, the sound of the radio and the sound of my own thoughts, the blood pumping through my brain.

He has the local news on. There is a short report about a search in lower Westchester for a missing teenage girl. It is a woman talking, very rapidly, as though out of breath, but in that fake way broadcasters have, where you know they are just acting upset and concerned—sounding concerned is part of their *job*. She says her name. She says, *"Hannah Scott is missing and the family fears the worst."* They say where her phone has been found, and ask for prayers for her family.

I sit and stare. Hannah, my friend, is the girl on the news. Her story is everywhere.

TWENTY-EIGHT

WHEN DAD AND I get home, I realize how much the world has changed.

It isn't only the radio; the local television station also has pictures of Hannah and the search that has spread across the county, since the cops put out the news that Hannah may not in fact have run away, that details in the case strongly suggest otherwise. Mom has the TV in the kitchen on as she chops vegetables and adds them to the pot on the stove, only she's not chopping onions and mushrooms so much as standing there with a knife in one hand and an untouched pile of shiitakes on the cutting board in front of her.

I can't take my eyes off the TV and the supposed "crime scene." The newscaster is a woman with long, windblown brown hair and a thin-lipped, grimacing mouth. Behind her you can see tall, wind-flattened clumps of cattails, and behind the cattails, the dark rising water of the Sound. I think how at low tide the preserve smells of decay, of the dead mussels and razor clams the seagulls peck out of shells sprung open on the large graffiti-covered rocks. Was it possible her phone was found out there because someone wanted it found? The preserve is a wild place, but it is not especially isolated. It is on the far side of the amusement park, as far from the entrance gates as the parking lot extends. But still, you could hit the pillars of the Dragon Coaster with a well-thrown stone from where the news lady is standing.

After dinner, I throw myself on my bed. For a minute or two I remain absolutely still. Then I take out my iPad and open the file labeled "Accountability." I *have* to get the letter finished. If I don't, I could lose ground with Group, and Chuck and I could become equals. I'd be humiliated, demoted if someone pointed out that my accountability letter was a day overdue. The group might even dismiss me, make me reapply and start back as a prospective. Somehow, failing in Group in front of Chuck seems even worse than failing all on my own.

I have a throbbing headache, but I start to type anyway. While I type, I think about Hannah. I think about her smile, her husky voice, her feral-cat way of standing and staring into a room, all boldness, showing no fear.

I look outside, into the dark. My window is open just a crack and there's a slight breeze. There is the smell of earth, not yet frozen. I think about Andy and I know he is also being pulled in two. I imagine how things are at his house tonight; I wonder where Jonas is, and what Andy's parents have found out.

I don't know where Hannah is. I don't have the missing piece of the puzzle. I just know how some of the pieces fit.

I sprawl across my white down comforter, start typing again and spill everything I know. I was wrong that I'm not accountable for telling what I know about Hannah. I kept her secrets when her secrets put her in danger. I'm responsible for that part.

The only thing I don't fess up to is sneaking around in order to meet Andy at Michiko's. This was a betrayal of trust like all the others, but there is something that feels wrong about adding it to the list. I know bad shit will keep happening to me as long as I am out of control about drinking. But even though Andy and I are both fuck-ups surrounded by even worse fuck-ups, I don't think we are wrong to need each other.

I take a break, toss my iPad behind me onto the pillow, and stretch. It's almost eleven, but the street has a kind of eerie glow to it. I go to the window and see the moon is full. It's so bright there are shadows on the sidewalk beneath the trees that still hold their red and yellow leaves. There was something on Mom's radio this morning, I remember now, about the moon being particularly close to Earth—closer than it'll be for another thousand years. I didn't think much of it at the time. It's like those meteor showers you're sure you're going to see, but you fall asleep, or it rains, or you just forget to look up. But the moon outside my window is closer, bigger, I think, than I've ever seen it before. It looms over the street in a weird way that makes me feel watched.

They say alcoholism is a disease, but I don't know. I think it's something else, like another law of physics, of the universe. There's just too much space, even in our own heads—there's too much emptiness, too much darkness. Something has to fill it: beer, vodka—anything that isn't nothing. That's the law—people are afraid to be nothing, and so we make ourselves *something*—drunk, beautiful, scary, anything that's real-seeming.

I shut my eyes and try to block out the too-bright, too-close moon.

Tomorrow, there's the lawyer, Group, and the police. Everywhere I go I'll be questioned.

I think how if this were a story, I'd know there was an end that I could skip to. But I know it's possible for a person to be lost and never found. I want to cry, not just because Hannah is missing, and I'm the friend who should have known what to do, but because there's no end to flip to, no certainty there ever will be. I let the tears run down my face. Somewhere, Hannah is beyond help, and I was the last one to hear from her, when she was still within reach.

There is a helicopter outside, maybe two, and they sound like they're flying low. I wonder if it's Hannah they're looking for. I shudder and stare out the window. The helicopter sounds soon fade. Maybe it was just the usual traffic jam on the interstate that drew them.

I change into my baggy gray sweats and an old Ether T-shirt and get into bed, just so I can tell myself this horrible day is over. The moment I shut my eyes, my body and mind sink into exhaustion. In just a few minutes, I'm nearly asleep. But as I'm about to drift off, my phone vibrates. It's a text from Andy. All it says is *Meet me by the red doors in the am*. I text back that I will and shut my eyes. I'm not supposed to have my phone in my room, but I keep forgetting to hand it over, and my parents keep forgetting to ask for it. That's the way it is with rules, I think. You have them so you don't get confused about how you're supposed to act. But then the rules are the first things everyone forgets.

TWENTY-NINE

MOM FRIES DAD'S usual eggs, drinking her coffee from her favorite flowered mug, as though this were a completely normal day. Dad sits at the table with his paper, sipping so loud I can hear it across the room. I wonder if there's an article about Hannah in the *New York Times*. Girls don't go missing every day, or maybe they do, but not in small, suburban towns like ours. Dad has the French doors open in the kitchen. I hear the whir of a helicopter again.

The silence in the room is awkward and tense. I feel nervous, and am having trouble focusing on everything I'm supposed to do in the next twelve hours, but I don't want to annoy Mom by complaining, so I go for some basic information.

"Mom, who's taking me to the Center today?" I ask. I think from the way she's dressed, it must be Dad. Her beige blouse and brown pants is an office look.

When she turns from the sink where she's washing Dad's

breakfast dishes, I can see she's either been crying or didn't get nearly enough sleep.

Dad puts his paper down. "I'm bringing you. Then, you're meeting with Barbara Fine and the detective tonight. You'll have an hour with Barbara first."

I nod.

"We'll get through this," Dad adds. I suppose this is true, but only because we have no choice. We hardly speak again. Even while Dad drives me to school, we're quiet. I want to hear some music, anything to break the silence, but I'm afraid to touch the radio. I'm afraid to do anything that I'm not being told to do.

When Dad drives off, I stand in front of the red doors waiting for Andy. People stream past. I don't look anyone in the face. I scan the crowd streaming across the parking lot, searching for Andy's goofy, loping stride, when I glimpse Senna ambling toward me. I have no choice but to face him.

"Marcelle," he says. "How you doing?"

"I'm okay, I guess," I mumble. "It's hard to deal with all this shit. . . ." I blink back tears and my voice sort of breaks when I try to say Hannah's name. Senna doesn't move. He stands next to me, crowding me, hands in his pockets. He stares over my head, squinting, as though looking for Hannah somewhere on the horizon.

"I wanted to join the people helping search, but my parents wouldn't let me go," Senna says. I'm shocked that Senna would say this, and that his parents had any say at all in what he did or did not do.

"They mentioned a search on the news," I say, "but there's no way my parents would let me go over there either." Senna nods, and to my surprise he seems reluctant to move on.

"I guess people think I'm, like, a suspect of some kind," Senna says abruptly. "Her boyfriend, you know, *numero uno* on the list." He pauses, then adds, "My parents hired me a lawyer." He gives me a long, questioning stare.

I look right into Senna's eyes. I try to see inside of him, to know what he's thinking, and I feel, weirdly, that he is doing the same with me. A person should be able to tell if another person is lying, or if they are hiding some awful truth, but I can't tell with Senna, and he doesn't seem to be able to tell with me, either.

"I thought about hitting the road," he says. "But I guess that would be the kiss of death." He pauses, looks down at his feet, then back at me again. "Do you think the cops really care if they get the right guy?" Senna asks.

I shake my head, dumbfounded. Senna doesn't seem angry, exactly; he's definitely worried. If he's trying to get me to feel sorry for him or afraid that the cops aren't to be trusted, he's succeeding. What if the cops decide we're all just a bunch of coke-dealing fuck-ups? What if they don't believe *my story*?

Then it hits me that Senna is assuming Hannah is dead. Senna is either assuming this, or he *knows* it.

I take a few deep breaths. When I regain my composure I tell him I have to run to class. I've forgotten all about Andy. But before I go, I say, "Maybe they're going to find her, Senna, and everything will be okay. Maybe there's a simple explanation."

I don't wait for an answer. I join the flow of kids heading toward the C building, and I see Senna moving in the opposite direction, but slowly, like someone wading through deep water. He stands head-and-shoulders above the crowd. He's easy to pick out until the end of the hallway, where he takes a sharp right, toward either the Spanish building or the parking lot. I breathe easier once he turns the corner and is finally out of sight. It's only then I think how strange it is that Andy didn't show up.

Math is longer than life itself, but I don't get called on, and am oddly able to concentrate on Mr. Hellman's lesson. I have the kind of clarity that comes from having so much on my mind I can only think about what's right in front of me.

Second period, I have Comp, during which I mostly think of Senna and everything I suspect but can't admit to myself. Ms. Bartow is giving us the whole period to revise our personal narratives. I mostly stare at mine. I make only a few tiny changes. I'm distracted by the fact that Andy isn't in class. Staring blankly across the room, it occurs to me that someone has taken Hannah's desk out of her row, so that every seat is taken but her row is one desk shorter now than all the others.

Finally, I have a free third period. Getting through the hallways is like swimming upstream. Everyone seems to be going in the opposite direction from me. I don't see faces, only bodies. Everywhere I go, I think I see Hannah. Glimpses of her hair— that color that is neither blond nor brown, but some sort of blend of both—a glimpse of her bare shoulder, but it's another girl who's doing that nineties off-the-shoulder thing. It's never Hannah. It's not her thin, tan leg. It's some other girl taking advantage of the warm day. I'm walking zombie-like through the crowd and everyone is staring at me because everyone knows about Hannah.

I finally get to the cafeteria. All I can think of is getting something hot to drink and having a minute to myself. I'll get a tea, then hang out in the freshman zone, where I'll be safe.

I push through the heavy doors of the cafeteria and immediately meet Andy's eyes. He's paying for his food behind a bunch of football players. They've all just shaved their heads in some team spirit effort. Andy looks thin and grim standing next to them, as they jostle each other and rub their hands over each other's smooth scalps. I think, *At least there's this distraction*. Everyone can talk about how hot Brian Housman still looks bald, or how Jeremy Caine is nothing without his flowing blond locks. At least some kids seem oblivious to the fact that Hannah Scott is missing, and that all night long the police from three towns have been searching the nature preserve for any sign of her.

Andy skipped Comp, but he knows I have third period free. He must have been watching the door, waiting for me.

He's a total mess. He staggers over to me with his coffee. Before I can say a word, Andy pulls me by my arm back out of the cafeteria. I'm annoyed, because I really need that tea, but I don't resist.

We walk, leaning into each other but not quite touching. Then I see it. Someone has written *Who killed that coke whore Hannah Scott?* on the side of the soda machine. I'm struck dumb. "Jesus," Andy says. He looks at me questioningly, as though I have any more idea than he does about who would write such a thing. Who actually hated Hannah enough to write something vicious like that?

"That's just what we need," Andy says. "Fucking gossips." He lets out a sigh and then shakes his head. I can see he's fighting back tears. We both simultaneously sit on the wide windowsill at the end of the hall.

He starts talking, head down, choking on his own words. "Cops came to my house last night. Asked my parents all kinds of questions about Jonas. They're getting me a lawyer." He pauses and then lets me have it. "Jonas was arrested." He exhales slowly. "Drug charges. Some guy at a convenience store saw the pic of Hannah, and said she'd been in there with Jonas. Guy knew Jonas by name. Police went over to Jonas's apartment and the fucking dumbass prick had shit all over the place." At this point Andy is crying. Two freshman girls walk by and grab on to each other as they catch wind of what Andy is saying.

Andy raises his coffee to take a sip, but then just stares at the muddy liquid. Did the cops consider Andy a drug dealer too? Andy must be thinking along these same lines, because his hands shake, spilling his coffee over the sides of the Styrofoam cup. He wipes his shirt cuffs on his jeans and shakes his head. He looks not just thin, but emaciated; his blue-and-gray flannel shirt hangs off him, as does the white T-shirt he has on underneath. Andy's the kind of guy who misses a single meal and evaporates.

"I'm sorry, Andy," I say. And I am, really sorry. I'm sorry for him and for me. I'm sorry for my parents and his, for Elise Scott, even Chuck's mom with her perfect hair and middle-of-the-day pumps. I want to blame Senna for everything, but is that fair? Or is it just because Senna scares me? I've never connected with Senna, but does that mean there's something actually wrong with the guy? Wrong enough that he'd hurt Hannah?

I put my hand on Andy's thigh. "What can I do, Andy?" I ask. "I want to help."

Andy rests his chin in his palm. I watch his face. I've never seen him like this. The ends of his eyelashes are damp with tears and his nose is running. His mouth is twisted-looking, and his cheeks are sunken in.

"They're going to ask you questions, Marci. They're coming to interview me, too. Just tell them what you know. It's what I'm going to do. Don't tell the others anything about Jonas. Senna, Chuck. Act like we didn't talk."

I move closer to Andy to signal he's the only one I trust. "Do you think Jonas will go to jail?" I half whisper. Andy shrugs. "I know he's my brother, and I messed up too, but if Jonas weren't such a lazy, greedy fuck, none of this would have happened. I wish he had just gone to college." Andy takes a sip of his coffee, then puts the cup down and buries his face in his hands. His hair is mussed on top, the ink-dark spikes dotted with dust. I want to tell him to go home, take a shower, get some sleep, but none of this is possible.

There's nothing I can say to Andy that will change anything. There's no way out but forward. Jonas is over eighteen, but Andy is only sixteen, and he really hasn't done much more than hook his friends up with his brother. But given the fact that Hannah is missing, it's doubtful any of us will get off easy. The best thing we can do, the only way we can help anyone, including ourselves, is by helping find out what happened to Hannah.

Kids start to spill out of the cafeteria and into the hallway. My free period is over and I have Spanish next. In another minute, the hallway will be packed with kids, and Andy and I will be swept along with the tide of people pushing and shoving, heading to class. I give Andy a squeeze on his thigh, and to my surprise he stands, pulls me up, and puts both his arms around me in a full-on hallway embrace. "I miss you," he mumbles into my neck, and holds me tight. I rest my head on his shoulder, not daring to move.

It feels useless to go to Spanish, but there's nothing else to do, and if I don't go, I'll be called out for cutting. I feel like everyone I pass is looking at me—the tiny freshman boys with huge backpacks, the long-haired senior stoners with their Phantasy T-shirts, the packs of sophomore girls whispering with their heads together. But are they really? Or is this some paranoid delusion?

A part of me wants nothing more than a cold six-pack of Heineken. I can almost picture myself hauling ass home, letting myself in the basement, and raiding Dad's beer fridge. But those days are over. Dad keeps his beer locked away. There's never more than one or two in the fridge.

Somehow, I get through Spanish and then the rest of the day. I don't see Andy or anyone else all afternoon until, miraculously, it's time for Dad to get me and take me to the Center. I stand in front of the guidance office with just my flannel over my T-shirt and overalls as the clouds gather and the air gets cooler. For once, I'm eager to get to the Center. I'm not thrilled that Chuck is there, but today the Center seems like the only place I'm likely to get the answers I need.

THIRTY

DAD PULLS UP to the building right at three, and his is the first car in the long line of parents picking up kids. I'm relieved that Dad is listening to the radio, and that it is not the local news but a public radio show about a controversial movie showing somewhere in the city. You can hear protestors in the background yelling. It sounds like chaos, but also like nothing. "Hey," Dad says, and shifts into drive. He gives me a cautious glance but says nothing more, and we drive out of the school parking lot in silence.

Finally, when we're out on the Post Road, I open up. My voice sounds strange and seems to come out of a deep, unknown place inside me. "I feel like a freak show, or a criminal," I say. "I feel like everywhere I go people are staring at me, like I should know something, like I *do* know something." I don't plan to say this, but the words fly out of my mouth. Dad slows the car.

"Did something happen?" He sounds stricken. What more

would need to have happened?

Then I tell him about the graffiti about Hannah. Dad doesn't say anything until we get into town and pull into the Center parking lot. He parks the SUV awkwardly, too close to the car next to us, and turns to me. "Listen very carefully," he says. "You do not speak to anyone. Anyone. About any of this until you speak to the lawyer Mom got you. Then, you do exactly what she says. Got it? She makes the decisions. Period." I sigh, wondering if I'll be able to squeeze out of the passenger-side door, or if I'll have to ask Dad to repark the car.

"Barbara Fine is my brain. I get it," I say. I'm not being a smart-ass. I'm trying to think. Dad shakes his head. No. His face darkens and his brows come together in concentration. He's trying to control himself. I wonder what it is he doesn't want to do—yell? Or actually slap me? I wouldn't blame him for either. Neither of my parents has ever hit me, but I almost want him to now. I want him to lose it on me. I want screaming, crying. I want mayhem. I want the rest of the world to feel like my own mind—fear-filled, confusion-filled, and inescapable.

Dad sighs, then speaks precisely. "Barbara Fine is an expert in criminal law and witness rights. You need her expertise. To get her expertise, she needs you to tell her everything you know. It's simple. Nothing you say to her will be repeated to us. Nothing is repeated to the police, or Elise Scott. Got it? You are not to decide what's relevant, good or bad, right or wrong. Above all, you don't say a thing to any of these people. These . . . friends of yours."

"I get it. I understand. It makes sense. Trust no one."

Every time I got drunk, I felt beautiful. Not like Hannah or a model in a magazine or a movie star, but like a tree or a mountain or the moon at night. I want to explain this to Dad, that I am good, deep down, and that what I want is simple, something anyone could understand.

For several minutes, Dad and I just sit there with the engine running, waiting. But the silence is not uncomfortable. I'm glad for it, and even thankful to him for not saying something to fill it.

Finally, I wipe my face on a crummy old tissue I find in the jacket pocket of my shirt, and I lean over and give Dad a kiss on the cheek. He says, "I'll be back by five thirty." I nod, and open the car door, which bangs into the blue Mercedes next to us. I've forgotten how close we are, and the door of the SUV has left a large white mark on the silver-blue sedan. I glance at Dad, who shakes his head and looks away while I squeeze myself through the space between the two cars.

At the Center, things are quiet. I say hi to James, who is pouring pretzels into a large lime-green plastic snack bowl. "Hey, Marcelle, how are you?" he says. I shrug. "Okay, I guess," I answer, remembering what Dad said in the car, about not talking about Hannah with anyone other than the lawyer. Did that mean here, too? I wonder. Did that mean I'm supposed to sit in Group and say nothing? It's not that easy, here, to keep quiet. Keeping quiet is actually sort of against the rules, and I have my accountability letter to present today—something I have to do, and that letter has to mention Hannah.

Down the hall, near the Group room, Cyndi is at the cubbies putting her book bag away and changing into her stupid fuzzy slippers. She leans over and pulls her hair to the side, so you can plainly see the half-shaved part. She has four gold hoops in one ear. I think she had an eyebrow piercing, too, but those aren't allowed at the Center. I wonder how Kevin feels about the snake tattoo Cyndi has coiled up her middle finger. That's something she can't undo.

It isn't only me. The other kids here have fucked up too. They have the scars, the tattoos, the angry, exhausted parents. But Cyndi, James, Ali, Martin, and even little Maria all have each other. James kicks people out of Group, but they come right back, or they come back after a day or two. Is accountability all about getting slapped down, then getting back up and trying again? Or is this all some kind of game, with kids like James and Cyndi acting self-important and everybody else just bouncing around, doing our time, waiting for someone to say we're okay again because we've done what we were told to, finally.

I smile faintly at Cyndi as I put my bag in my cubby. Cyndi's cubby is decorated with stickers with sober-living messages like *One Day at a Time*, *Easy Does It*, and *Do the Next Right Thing*. My cubby doesn't even have my name on it yet, and it won't until I get my accountability letter accepted by the Group. I pull my black-and-white marbled notebook out of my book bag. Last night, I printed out my accountability letter and slipped a copy in the front of my journal. I check to make sure it's still there. I can't afford not to be on top of things today. Cyndi barely looks my way. So far, there is no sign of Chuck. What will it mean, I wonder, if Chuck doesn't show up? What will it mean if he does?

Kevin is in his office with the door open, calling something out to James, who is still in the kitchen. I envy the way James and Cyndi are so at home here. I'm supposed to have a check-in with Kevin again this week, since I bombed my last one, but I haven't scheduled anything so far. I have to start *initiating*. Initiating in Center lingo is doing what you're supposed to without someone telling you. I'm supposed to be able to figure out what's important on my own. I've always been bad at this.

I pause outside Kevin's office, unsure what to say. He looks up. His eyes have a strange intensity. The brown part is too bright, and there is too much white altogether. "Hey," I say quietly. Kevin doesn't say anything back, but waits for me to go on. "I think I need a check-in," I say.

Kevin stops what he's doing and eyes me. I know I'm doing this all wrong. "You think you do, or you know you do? You want to, or you think you're supposed to want to?" He's not speaking in an angry way, but I feel like I have tripped over an invisible wire.

"I need to?" I say. Then I correct myself. "I mean, I know it's part of the program to do it, but I would also like to speak to you." Kevin nods. Then he gestures toward the sign-up sheet taped to his office door. Why did no one ever point this out to me? Everything at the Center is supposed to be done a certain way, but no one ever says how or why. It's like a scavenger hunt. It's like somewhere in that building they've hidden all the clues to getting through the program, for being sober, for finding meaning in an empty universe, but you have to put the pieces together alone.

I sign up on Kevin's sheet for a meeting tomorrow. This is an eternity. By tomorrow, Hannah will be found, I tell myself. If she isn't, I'll have to live with all of my questions, all of my fears, and all of my regrets, maybe for the rest of my life. I'll have to go on anyway.

I push Hannah and Andy and the meeting tonight with Barbara Fine out of my mind. That's what I do now. I get through stuff, not big stuff like days, but small stuff, like minutes.

"But Marcelle?" Kevin stops me. "Love to have you sign up for a meeting, but you're in as of today. James, Cyndi, and I all approve the AL you posted last night. You can talk about it when they call on you today in Group." I breathe a sigh of relief.

Chuck must have gotten here while I was in Kevin's office. He sits next to James, drinking a Coke. Maria sits at the end of the table with her owlish eyes and narrow chin poking out of a black turtleneck. She has on leggings and she curls up, cat-like, in her seat. For the first time she looks like a teenager to me and not a child.

Martin starts the meeting off. He's next to Cyndi, slouched down, eyes half shut. He looks at Cyndi before he begins, and she nods, like she knows all about whatever he's going to say. I feel angry for no particular reason. Maybe it's just Cyndi, and the way she runs the meeting. At least James sometimes smiles.

Martin clears his throat twice. "I guess I just have to fess up," he says. He's almost crying. We're supposed to give each other eye contact at the table, but it's too painful for me to watch Martin dissolve. Martin struggles to get his words out.

"I fucked up yesterday, for real. I didn't go right home after Group, like I was supposed to. I knew no one was there. I went to a bro's house, instead, guy I used to hang with. I knew it was kind of a problem that I was going there, and I didn't really check in with myself about what I was doing, and a bunch of other guys were there doing bong hits, and someone passed the bong to me." He stops, takes a sip of his Sprite. "So that's it, man. I don't know why I did it. Couple other times I hung out and let it go, but something about being with this particular brother, you know, I didn't care about anything. I blew it."

There is a heavy silence.

James narrows his eyes at Martin. My heart pounds. I start to sweat. I hardly know Martin, and yet I feel myself begin to panic for him.

"You know what you've got to do?" James says. Martin nods, and a large tear forms in the corner of his right eye and slides down the smooth dark of his cheek. "Checking outta this joint," Martin says with a nod. "But I'm coming back." He stares at Cyndi, and I wonder about the two of them, once again. Dating each other is against Center rules, but there's clearly something simmering there. "It was a slip," Martin says. "That's all. A fucking slip." Martin pushes the door open hard so that it bangs the outside wall on his way out.

Martin's main issue was Percocet. He got caught dealing, but just by his school and parents, so he isn't mandated by the court to be here. He told me his story one of my first days at the Center, how his dad found his stash of weed and fake Percs he got online when his prescription for his football injury ran out. That night, his Dad grabbed him by the shirt collar and slammed him against the wall, not once, but three times, until Martin was actually scared, breathless, until his mom threatened to call the police. Then his mom hit the internet and found the Center. He's been coming to the Center since June, sober the whole time.

Cyndi looks around the room. "Wow," she says, shaking her head. "That was fucking hard." I stare across the table and catch Chuck's eye, but I can't tell what he's thinking. Maybe he has too much on his mind to care about the drama unfolding in front of us. In spite of everything, I want Martin to come back. I hate the idea of anyone else I know disappearing.

James looks thoughtfully at the door. "He's coming," he says cryptically.

The door opens quietly, and then Martin, tears on his face, works his way back around the table, pulls out his chair, sits down, and folds his arms in front of him.

"A. Fucking. Slip," Martin says. "That's it. I didn't have to say anything about it. I came clean. It's not happening again. I'm in control. That's it."

James and Cyndi exchange glances and I think I see a shadow of a smile on James's face. Cyndi, though, is all chin up and staring straight at Martin. Maybe she's proud of her man, putting up his fight. I'm waiting, getting more anxious by the second. The longer the Martin show takes, the longer I have to wait to give my own accountability talk, the speech that tells the world just what sort of fucked-up people my friends, including Chuck Glasser, really are.

Cyndi sighs. "Martin, you know the rule. This is a zero-tolerance program. One strike and you're out. You need to sign your release papers. You can reapply when you're approved. It'll be really fast, if you do it right, I'm sure of it."

Martin shakes his head. "No can do. I belong here. I fucked up, I know that, but this is my place." He sits up straight and opens his notebook, and puts his hand under his chin in an elaborate show of attentiveness.

"Yo," Ali interrupts. "Man, I can see where you're coming from, and I've got your back one hundred percent, but you are jeopardizing your return right now. You gotta pack it in, do your time, and we'll be here for y'all."

There's silence around the table. I want to scream at the whole group of them to listen to me, to my story. But at the Center we don't freak out and put our shit ahead of anyone else's shit, and for now we are stuck on Martin, who still hasn't budged.

The tension in the room is electric. I think someone will finally run out and get Kevin, get Security, but that's not what happens next. It never ceases to amaze me how alone we are in here, in this room. How in charge of things James and Cyndi really seem to be.

"Okay," James says. "I'm calling a vote on Disrespect." This is one of those things in the back pages of the Center manual that I didn't really think I'd ever see. A vote on Disrespect is like the death penalty at the Center. It's the nuclear option. You can basically reapply after shooting up, after going on a weeklong binge. You go back through intake and probation and Account-ability and Goals all over again. But if they vote you out on Disrespect, that's it. You can't come back. Ever.

Martin sits stone-still. "All at the table who vote Martin for a Disrespect card, please raise your hand," James says, while immediately raising his own. Ali, reluctantly, raises his hand as well, his face a mask of grief; Cyndi, poker-faced, raises hers; then Chuck, looking pale, but maybe a little confused about whether he is supposed to even vote, raises his hand too. Then little Maria raises her pale, skinny arm.

I am the only one not voting against Martin. I can't. My hand just won't go up. I'm the last person to want to stand out from the crowd, but I can't seem to follow along. I also want nothing more than to get beyond the Martin crisis, and since Disrespect is a unanimous decision, I am the one holding every-thing up. But I've done nothing my entire life but go along with what everyone else is doing, sit in admiration for the other kids who seem smarter, prettier, or more self-assured than me. But what if they aren't? What if the other kids here, including Cyndi and James, are the same as me—just dumb, fucked-up kids doing the best they can?

I know the Center has rules, and they are supposed to apply to everyone equally, and zero tolerance is our biggest, most important rule ever, but I can't pretend to understand pushing Martin out. It seems cruel to make him leave, confess repeatedly, and reapply. To tell him he can never come back just seems horrible. I imagine him going home and his dad screaming at him and his mother's silent fury. I imagine the whole scene, and I want to go up and hug Martin. I am tired of angry, disappointed people. I don't want to push Martin back down into the hell I've been living in, the hell of everyone looking at you like you're the bomb that's about to explode.

James stares at me. "Marcelle? You're not in favor of a vote of Disrespect?"

I shake my head. "No," I say. "No, I'm not. I know I'm new," I whisper, "but I don't think Martin is showing a disrespect for the rules."

"Marcelle, he . . ." Cyndi starts to disagree, but James raises his hand to silence her.

"Go on," he says.

"Well, I know we're a zero-tolerance program, and we have all sworn off drug use. But I think Martin came to us for help. I don't see him disrespecting the rules by asking for a second chance. I think he's being brave and asking for us to help him stay on track. So I think he's doing everything he can in this situation. Maybe he should reapply, I can't say about that. But I don't see disrespect going on. I know what the manual says about slips, but even in the real world people sometimes bend the rules. People sometimes go with their instincts. They have sympathy. They care about people. I think Martin learned something when he messed up. Like now he really knows he wants to be here. Like he actually knows why he's here and what this Group is really for."

The Group is silent. Martin shakes his head in disbelief. I'm in shock, myself. It's like I've split in two, and there's the Marcelle who is sitting here, as usual, just hoping things will go my way, but there's a new Marcelle, too, who's sick of other people controlling everything. The new Marcelle has taken possession of my voice.

THIRTY-ONE

FOR A MINUTE I'm afraid James will turn on me—that I've said or done something that will get me tossed from Group along with Martin. But James doesn't miss a beat. It's like there's nothing he isn't prepared for. "Okay," James says. "Since our Disrespect vote has failed, and Marcelle does not see Martin's actions as equaling Disrespect, I rescind the vote. Martin's slip will be noted in our official minutes and submitted to Kevin for review. Let's take a five-minute break before we go on, then we have Accountability Group." I start to ask James where I should sit for my accountability talk, but then to my surprise, Chuck interrupts.

"Actually, I got my letter in last night at around seven," Chuck says. "So I think I'm up before Marcelle." I only voted Chuck in yesterday. This means he has been working on his accountability letter and his Personal Goal Plan since before he was even voted in. I think this must be some sort of procedural error, something that would warrant Chuck taking two giant steps back. But I just took the whole group on over Martin. I can't take Chuck on now too, and James and Cyndi are nodding, and have clearly accepted Chuck's letter. I've been in English class with Chuck. I know he's got skills and can write a five-page paper in an hour class, so I have no problem believing he's gotten the letter done. Still, it seems like cheating somehow. What does Chuck even understand about this place? About being sober?

I look around the table. Cyndi and James, Ali, Martin, Maria, everyone seems focused on Chuck. Accountability letters are complicated. There are about ten different guidelines. Once your letter is accepted, you are on to the next phase of the program where the real work is. James told me my first day here that he rewrote his accountability letter three times. Cyndi rewrote hers a staggering nine times. You are really supposed to expose not only everything you think you *did* wrong, but also all your fucked-up ways of thinking about other people. It's not something you can fake. The fact that Chuck wrote his and got it accepted gives me pause. Maybe Chuck really is here for himself. If so, I'm more confused than ever about who Chuck Glasser really is.

It doesn't matter that Chuck got his accountability letter in before me. Whatever else the Center is doing or not doing for me, I'm learning I need to be heard. I've always hidden my thoughts, even from my closest friends, if I thought they'd disagree with me, even about little stuff, like music I enjoy, or teachers I like. Getting drunk is a really big way of hiding. It's a way of hiding from the inside out. Whatever Chuck has to say, he can't stop me from telling my story here. I peer across the table at Martin. I saved Martin's ass. Senna and Chuck might think I'm still poor, pathetic, drunk Marcelle. But I'm not that girl. Not anymore. It's not that I think I'll never fuck up again. Fucking up is a part of who I am. But like Martin, I'm not afraid to lay it on the line. I'm proving that to myself, right now, at this table. I stood up for Martin. I said what I thought.

Chuck stands behind his chair. He clears his throat and scratches his perfect chin. Everyone is silent. He has a few double-sided, typed pages in his hand. Lots of writing. But he puts the letter down on the table in front of him. You don't have to read your whole letter to the Group when you stand for account-ability. You just have to talk about it, and the Group leaders have a copy, so they can ask you about anything they want. But Chuck puts his letter facedown on the table, like it has nothing to do with what he's about to say. "It was me," Chuck says. He says this in a quiet voice, and no one but me seems to catch it. He stands up straighter and says it again, a little louder this time. "It was me. I killed Hannah. Or I might as well have."

I hear my voice before I know I am making a sound. I am saying "No, no, Chuck." I don't believe what I'm hearing. I real-ize I never really believed any of it. It was like I had been asleep for days, and this had been a bad dream, a nightmare, but sud-denly it's real and Hannah is dead. A million thoughts rush through my mind. It's impossible to imagine. Hannah was a little girl when we met, just eleven and only four feet something. Her backpack was too big on her back. She had her hair dyed blue and she wore blue mascara to match. She was a crazy little girl bounding on the trampoline behind her house, blue hair wrapping around her neck as she flipped and flipped and flipped.

No. Take it back. You didn't.

I choke out a sob. It's Martin who comes to me, puts his arms around me, and lets me fall, crying, into his arms.

This is real. This is not real.

Martin pulls an empty chair over, scoots next to me, and lets me lean into him. I grab on to his arm, his shoulder, his shirt, as Chuck stands and waits. Everyone else is frozen. Cyndi is expressionless. James looks confused, crumpled somehow from within. Ali is standing half out of his seat. Maria stands away from the Group table with her hand on the door. It makes sense, we should all be running. We should all rush out of the building together and run for help.

But the story isn't over yet. Everyone is as confused as I am. Obviously, Chuck didn't write any of this in his letter. If he had, he wouldn't be here right now.

But why is he here, spilling his guts to us? Group is confidential. No one is supposed to be able to say anything to anyone about what they hear in this room, just like in a doctor's office, or with a therapist. But this must be different, I think. This is someone's life. I try to focus. I need to hear what Chuck is saying despite the blood roaring in my ears. I need to understand what is happening.

Chuck, hunched, thin, wild-eyed, biting his full bottom lip between words, continues his story.

"She came to my house Sunday after lunch. My parents were out, and she stayed all day," Chuck began. "We smoked, hung around, slept." He speaks in a dark monotone. So, he and Hannah were together, behind Senna's back, a dangerous move in itself, but not something I didn't see coming. I knew he wanted her back.

"I knew they were coming home from seeing my uncle in New Jersey." He pauses and breathes. "He has this thing wrong with his leg, some sort of tumor, so they help out. My sister went too." We all nod, like this part about New Jersey helps us understand something crucial about what happened. There is a sick uncle. No one does the usual stuff, like soccer practice or grocery shopping.

"That's when Hannah texted you," he says. He looks directly at me, implicating me. "Because she didn't want to go home, and Senna kept texting, but she wanted out of all that. She wanted to get away from him and all the shit he'd gotten her into. We were just talking at that point."

"Then she said she wanted to go for a walk up by the reservoir, even though it was already dark. So we walked over there, by the summer camp. We hiked up a while and then went off the trail to a place I know from when I was little." Chuck's family lives near these woods. There are paths all through them, most leading nowhere—someone's backyard, back to the same trail, down to the water's edge where people walk their dogs and jog on the wide gravel path. I can picture these places in my mind, even though it's been years since I've been there.

"We went to this cool place where there's a big, flat rock next to an old shed, so no one could see us. We put down a blanket. I didn't want to do anything, but then she opened her bag and pulled out her wrap. At first I said no, that the two of us should quit and get sober, like Marcelle. Things had gotten too crazy. But she started kissing me and doing other stuff, getting me into it, so I couldn't think. Then she said we would get sober, but later, after this one time, because she had this really intense shit, and she wanted to do it with me, alone."

I suddenly feel even sicker, chilled, my legs shaking. Martin puts his hand on my thigh, stilling me. I need to listen. I need to know this story.

"She had a mirror and a blade. She laid out a few lines. We did them and then talked some more. She was upset. She was talking about Alex and how he'd trapped her. About this webcam shit she did, and how it was supposed to be just a few times, just to pay for her stash. But then he wanted her to do more—to just keep on doing it, because she was really popular. All these guys are really into her—this hot young girl." Chuck sighs. He's looking around for a drink. Someone hands him his Coke. It's Maria. She's crept back to her seat next to Chuck. She's not afraid anymore. The story has taken a familiar turn. This is not about murder. This is about drugs. This is about the same wave that knocked every one of us into the obliterating dark.

Oh, Chuck, I think. *Even you couldn't stop her.* Was she that strong? Or was she so weak, she couldn't hold on no matter how many hands reached out for her?

"I didn't really want to do any more of that shit. It had a nasty aftertaste, made me feel weird, like numb in my throat. But Hannah kept laying the shit out. She wanted to talk. Do blow and talk. She has these moods." He looks right at me when he says this. *Yes*, I nod, *she has these moods*. Hannah the talker, the singer, the dancer. Hannah the unstoppable.

"She kept saying she wanted to be done with it all. With Senna and these guys. That maybe she needed rehab. Which she did. She really did. Because the lines kept getting spilled out, and she kept at it. So I did a couple more lines. Then we just lay there, talking, with the night getting darker. My parents were calling, looking for me. Senna was after her. We turned off our phones. I stopped caring at some point. It got later and later. She did a little more blow, then all of a sudden she said she should get going. She messed with her things, still doing lines so she could get home, study a little, maybe pull an all-nighter, getting shit done. And that's when it happened.

"She was standing up after doing a fat line off the back of her little mirror and her nose started to bleed and she was coughing. Then she started shaking a little all over. I told her to lie down and she did. She got next to me, but the shaking didn't stop. She was having a hard time breathing. I started feeling something too, then, like short of breath. But she was gurgling, choking kind of, and shaking, and she started to turn a weird color. I looked for my phone in the dark, but I was pretty fucked up and everything started flashing, like there was lightning, only there wasn't any. My hands were shaking, and finally I felt the phone under the blanket. I turned it back on and I started to dial 911, but I couldn't get it right. It was like in a dream where you keep trying to do some simple thing, but you can't. I tried maybe two, three times. But then I looked over at her and she was perfectly still. She had a little spit on her face, but she wasn't shaking anymore.

"That's when I totally freaked. I shook her. I hit her. I hit her really hard in the face, trying to wake her up. But I was also really mad, just, like, furious because she wouldn't listen to me. The whole fucking day I was trying to save her, tell her I love her, and she wouldn't listen."

Chuck is hunched over like something is wrong with his stomach. He rocks back and forth in his chair. Maria kneels beside him now, but still no one interrupts.

"She was so stupid. I didn't understand. How could she love that fat psycho fuck? Let him do that to her? But then I stopped being mad, and I started getting scared all over again. Terrified. Too scared to think.

"I realized, looking at her, that the shit we did was cut with something bad, some kind of poison. That's why it had that weird taste. I figured whatever it was, that shit was in my brain. I was losing my mind. I was going crazy on this poison shit and hitting this dead girl—Hannah. So I went through her stuff, cut lines out of the rest of her wrap and I did it all. Then I ran around for, like, an hour in the woods. Waiting for it to take me, too. But it didn't.

"When I got back to where I'd left her, she looked awful. I was so scared. I almost shit right there. I wanted to die. I really did.

"The little place we were hanging out, by that shed, isn't easy to see from anywhere. It's way in back of all the houses, where that summer camp had a shooting range. I kicked some leaves over her. Then I ran home. I figured when I got in I'd do something. Call the cops, 911. I wasn't sure what. I figured my dad would be up waiting to kick the shit out of me. It was late, like four in the morning. But the house was dark.

"There was no one to talk to, tell this crazy shit to. If my parents had been around I'd have just screamed the whole thing out, but they weren't, and I was still high as fuck. I figured the only way forward was to fucking just do it. Off myself. So with all that shit in my system, I ran into the bathroom and took whatever else I could find. But all we had was Tylenol, Motrin, cold medicine. I still took whatever I could get my hands on. I figured it would work if I took enough.

"But I just got sick. I was throwing up all over the sink, the bathtub. I don't know how long that went on, but finally I passed out. That's how my sister found me the next morning."

Everyone is silent. No one moves. But there is something wrong. Chuck's story makes a kind of sense. I know Chuck. He's impulsive. But I'm still confused.

"Wait," I say. "What about her phone?"

Chuck looks up. Shrugs. "I had it in my pocket. When I was trying to call for help, I must have grabbed both our phones, but I was too fucked up to realize it. Monday, I still went to school, mostly because I was too scared to be alone in my house. My sister helped me clean the bathroom. My mother and father were out early. No one knew but my sister how fucked up I'd been. When I saw you Monday, Marcelle, I thought for sure you knew something, and that you'd ask me where she was, but it was like you felt guilty about covering for her, or you just didn't want to talk to me, and that's the way it's been ever since with you. Senna was convinced she was with Alex, the guy she was doing the webcam shit for. Senna said he would kill the guy. Then, he was, like, Hannah wasn't worth the time, that she was nothing to him now, just a stupid coke whore who was going to make him pay for her bullshit.

"I drove over to the beach in Rye after school on Monday. I thought about just walking into the Sound until the water came over my head. I even started walking in, but it was low tide. You can walk across the whole fucking Sound all the way to Long Island when the tide is low. So I left. I threw her phone into the reeds out behind the amusement park and got back into my car."

Chuck stops. His face looks bloated, misshapen, as though his awful words are deforming him as he says them.

I know Hannah as well as anyone. I can grasp everything Chuck is saying. I can see it in my head, like a movie. How she died. How angry he had gotten. I could almost see myself being angry at Hannah like that, for dying, for being so stupid, for not loving the right people, for loving being high more than anything else.

But, somehow, the fact he threw her phone away in the preserve turns my blood cold. It leads me to the next question: How could he leave her there? Make everyone believe she was somewhere else? Cover himself and hope the cops and everyone else thought she'd run away, when she was there in the woods, when her body was a mile or so from his house, day and night? Then he comes here instead of to the cops, knowing we aren't supposed to tell anyone. It makes me furious. Chuck supposedly loved Hannah, but he was willing to leave her body to rot. Chuck Glasser is as bad as Alex, or worse. Then he comes here, like a coward, to absolve himself.

Then I think of something else that doesn't make any sense. Why had no one found her? There must be a smell. . . . I think of the times I've ridden the Death Wish and how even a tiny dead animal, a mole or a mouse, could stink up the whole trail. It has been warm all week. I haven't worn anything heavier than my flannel. Today is the first day it's been the least bit chilly.

Martin sits at my side, rubbing my back. Maria stands next to Chuck. Cyndi, James, and Ali all stare at Chuck in silence. Chuck looks broken. His eyes are red. His nose runs. I want to scream at him. I want to pound his chest with my fists. The silence in the room feels thick and suffocating.

Finally, James speaks.

"Okay, let's take a deep breath. I think we all are in agreement that this group is a confidential one?" He looks around and to my shock everyone nods. I feel my back stiffen and Martin squeezes my shoulder hard, like he's giving me a signal.

We all signed a confidentiality agreement. We all broke laws. Martin had his drugs. Maria had nearly starved herself to death, and hoarded shoplifted laxatives to do it. James and Cyndi were both junkies. Maybe they knew kids who died? Had either of them watched a friend OD? Maybe they'll want to protect Chuck.

Cyndi backs James up. "I can see why people are upset by Chuck's confession," she says. "Especially you, Marcelle. But none of us are responsible for Chuck's actions. Only Chuck can make amends." I'm grateful she says this, although she avoids looking at me as she speaks. Then she adds, "It's for Chuck to come clean. It's for this group to support Chuck in his contin-ued sobriety and in his work toward an honest, sober life."

When Cyndi finishes, Chuck, pale and hollow-eyed, nods but says nothing. Then he stuffs his papers into his book bag, like he's got someplace to be. I think, *Good, he's getting out of here, turning himself in.* But then Martin raises his hand.

"Martin," James says. "You've got something?"

"Yeah," Martin says. "I thought we were doing Marcelle today, too."

Everyone stares. Despite James's and Cyndi's composure during Chuck's confession, I think we were all figuring that was it for today. But Martin is right, at least on one count. It is only four thirty. We have forty-five more minutes of Group.

"Huh?" James says, looking at the clock. Cyndi is already turned toward me expectantly, on to the next drama. Chuck is ashen-faced. Ali and Maria both look close to tears, traumatized by Chuck's story. There is something wrong here. Someone needs to do something. We can't just go on as though Chuck's confession is just another piece of Group business. Hannah is dead.

THIRTY-TWO

I GLANCE AT James, who nods, and I open my notebook. I take out my typewritten pages. James nods again. "Okay, guys, I know this has been a really heavy meeting already. Let's have a minute of silent meditation. Let's let Chuck take his load from our shoulders. Let's take back only the burdens that are ours."

We do it. We sit in silence, each one of us staring down at our own hands. At the end of the minute, everyone turns back to me. Weirdly, they all actually look more comfortable than before James spoke his incantation, as if Chuck's burdens really were lifted from us all. I smooth out my pages.

"If I were a good friend, Hannah would be alive," I say.

I have their attention.

"I believe Chuck's story, that she OD'd or had some reaction to the blow she and Chuck did. That actually happened before. Where she shook like that. Jonas said maybe Hannah was allergic to something they mixed their blow with. It happened maybe a few weeks ago, when she and I were at Senna's. It didn't happen to anyone else, just her."

"So, you think you should have known the girl was going to ignore her own body and keep binging like that?" Cyndi interrupts. This is a total breach. She is supposed to let me finish my whole accountability presentation before any kind of question. James shoots her a look like she's lost her mind and she flushes, embarrassed.

"No," I say, shaking my head. "It's just one thing. I mean, a lot of us were there—Senna, Andy, and Andy's brother, Jonas. Any of us could see she was taking a risk. No," I begin again. "I mean, I should have gotten help, gone to my parents, or to her mom as soon as I knew what she and Senna were doing with Alex. She was ruining her life. Hannah kept saying she knew what she was doing. I wanted to believe her. But now I think I just didn't want to get everyone in trouble."

I take a deep breath.

Martin gets up, walks across the room, and grabs the tissue box from the bookshelf and brings it to me. "But she didn't know what she was doing, really. She had just stopped caring," I say. "It didn't matter to her how anybody saw her. We kind of fought about it, but I backed down. I didn't say she was wrong. It does matter. What other people see is who you are."

I stare at Chuck because this is where he came in, when Hannah stopped trying to save herself. Before the night he left her there for dead, I had turned away from her, too. It was like something inside of Hannah had died, and I hardly knew her anymore, or maybe nobody did; maybe she was just unknowable. I turned away because I was afraid.

"I knew these guys could make Hannah do just about anything, because she didn't have the money to be doing what she was doing. She was lost, and I gave up on her. Chuck and I are the same," I say. "We both ran away and tried to die."

"I used alcohol—beer and vodka—to silence my own thoughts. I thought I couldn't live with myself sober. I knew my friendship with Hannah was just another kind of loneliness. Even when we were together, we were both chasing our own highs. I don't know what being high was for her. But for me it was about forgetting—forgetting with my mind and my body. I wanted to live in some other world, not this one. I wanted my life to feel good, not be good. I don't really know what a good life is, but I think that's okay right now, even though it scares me. I'm sixteen. There's a lot of stuff I don't know still.

"I know I wasn't a good friend to Hannah. I want to think about that—about how I could be different. How maybe the next time, if there is a next time, that someone I'm close to can't do it—can't hold it together anymore—and I see that, I hope I'm brave enough to help them. I hope I'm brave enough to say no when that's what needs to be said. I hope I can see clearly next time. I hope I can make myself heard. I hope I'm never again the person who does nothing but watch. I hope *that* Marcelle is dead. I think being here, being in this Group, has taught me that one thing. I can't be someone with nothing to say." My voice breaks. "That's it. That's all I have."

Everyone is quiet. I hear sniffling and think Martin may be crying next to me, but I'm afraid to look and catch his eye. To my surprise, it's tiny Maria who breaks the silence. She raises her white doll hand, which dangles on her marionette wrist. James nods for her to speak.

"How do you know your friend Hannah wasn't deliberately poisoned?" Maria asks.

Cyndi shakes her head. "We aren't here to play kid detectives. It's not a game. Let the adults do their jobs." Maria looks taken aback for a moment, and turns to me with her wide, innocent eyes. Chuck will confess to Perez. He has to. What will happen to him, I don't know.

There's an army of cops looking for Hannah. It's only a matter of time before they find her. And what Maria says doesn't ring true to me. No one wanted her dead. Alex and Senna wanted to use her.

A part of me wants to shake Chuck and make him call the cops right now. I desperately wish Kevin was in his office, but on Thursdays he leaves at the start of Group for his private practice—it's just kids in the Center on those afternoons, with the security guy, Joseph. I want someone to make things clear and right, to spell out the rules about confidentiality, to explain what, if anything, Chuck did that might get him arrested.

"Okay," James says, looking around the room. Everyone sits stone-still. "I think that will have to be it for today," he continues. "We've heard Marcelle and Chuck's Accountability talks. If we have more questions for Chuck or Marcelle, we can ask them tomorrow, or whenever we see them next."

We file out of the Group room in silence. I'm at the front of the line. I want to linger and talk to Martin, but I don't want to end up face-to-face with Chuck. I stop and get my things from my cubby and head toward the exit, when I hear a snippet of conversation between Maria and Chuck. "But Chuck," Maria says in her small, chirpy voice, "how could you tell that the girl was really dead?"

Chuck replies mysteriously, "I saw her go." He says it as though she'd left a party, as though there had been a doorway he saw her pass through, and then an emptiness once she'd gone.

THIRTY-THREE

WHEN DAD PICKS me up, I'm exhausted. My legs ache and my neck feels stiff. It's foggy and he has the windshield wipers on.

I gaze out the window. Hannah is out there. I know where she is, or at least where Chuck says he left her. *Chuck has to tell the police what he did*, I tell myself. He has to tell them what he told us: that he watched Hannah die. I'll meet with my lawyer as soon as I get home. I'll tell her what I know, and what I heard from Chuck. My chest aches so bad I think it's true what they say—hearts *do* break. Who knows why? I only know I'll never forget this searing pain. I picture Hannah alone in the darkness—I think how she's been out there night after night—her poor body, a few leaves kicked over it, as if she were nothing—as if her life never meant anything to anyone.

"So how you holding up?" Dad asks.

"I don't know," I say, too softly for him to hear. He pulls into the driveway, puts the car in park, and lets out a heavy sigh. I don't know what to say. I don't know how to explain what I've just heard. My parents know only that I drank too much. They know nothing of the drugs my friends have been doing. How do I tell my father I know where Hannah's body is because Chuck Glasser watched her overdose in the woods by the reservoir Sunday night?

We sit there in silence until a black Porsche pulls in behind us. I assume this is the lawyer, Barbara Fine.

As soon as Dad and I get into the house I run upstairs to the bathroom. My stomach is in knots, and at first I think I'll puke, but instead I have the runs. I hear Mom and Dad greet Barbara Fine. On the toilet, I start to cry even harder. I think for sure they will hear me but no one comes up. After about five minutes of gagging and shitting, I leave the bathroom. I wash my hands and face, sure some putrid odor clings to me.

When I get downstairs, Barbara Fine and my parents are sitting across from each other in the living room. Barbara Fine sits with her knees pressed together. She speaks to my father in a deep, quiet voice. She could be fifty or sixty, I can't tell. She's heavyset with gray hair in a poofy, combed-back, old-lady 'do. Her neck has neck wattle. But her eyes are like the eyes of a cat, bright green and slanted.

Mom introduces me. Barbara Fine fixes me in her gaze. Her skin is pale, almost translucent. She has a large, hooked nose and a pert mouth. I trust her instantly.

After we shake hands and sit, Mom and Dad leave. At first,

I just cry. Barbara Fine says nothing. She waits a minute or two, then pats me on the knee, indicating it's time to pull myself together.

I take a deep breath, and I barely pause until I tell Barbara Fine everything, including the part about Alex grabbing me at his apartment, and how I froze then and could think of no way to defend myself. I tell her about the webcam business, the coke, and how Hannah and Senna failed to make any money, how they just sold enough to buy more coke. Once I finish my whole story, including Chuck's confession at the Center, she purses her lips thoughtfully and asks me to repeat a lot of what I've already said. She takes notes as I speak and shakes her head occasionally. She doesn't seem particularly shocked by any of it, although her eyes widen at the part about the porn site and narrow when I tell her about Chuck.

"And Marcelle, on how many occasions were you present when your friend was performing for this webcam?"

I shake my head. "Never," I say.

"So, it is just the wig and Hannah's own account of this business?"

"Yes," I say.

"Okay," she says. "And were you present when these meetings with Andy's brother took place? Their cocaine connection?"

I shake my head. "Not really. I was around when Jonas delivered stuff, and when Alex came to Senna's, but I stayed away from Alex after the first night at his place."

"Well, everything you tell me is privileged, so I can't go to the police with the information from Chuck. But you need to," she says after a moment.

"But what about the Group?" I ask. "James and Cyndi say everything there is confidential."

"That, my dear, is a load of bullcrap. Just irresponsible to put those misguided kids in charge of each other. What is this place? Sounds like something out of *Lord of the Flies*. Loads of legal precedent here—like that gentleman arrested on a rape charge twenty years after the fact, after he came clean at AA!" I have no idea what she's talking about, but I am relieved she does. Gradually, I feel my stomach begin to settle.

"You know, there's one other thing. Something Maria said that I overheard."

"Yes?" she asks.

"Well, on our way out of Group, Maria asked Chuck how he even knew Hannah was dead when he left her. And I started thinking, why *didn't* anyone smell her? These dogs or people who run by there? I was thinking just now, what if? What if she's just there? Alive, but she can't move? Like in a coma? What if Chuck is wrong and we're sitting here talking and she's out there alone, alive?"

Barbara Fine stares hard at me for a second, raises her finger, then rests her hand on my shoulder and takes out an ancient flip phone.

Detective Perez arrives at our house a half hour later along with the dark-haired guy, Connelly. It takes an hour and a half for me to tell my story while Perez sits nodding and writing.

Up close, his eyes are a yellowish-brown and he's much younger than I thought, maybe only in his late twenties. He calls me "honey." When I get to what Chuck said at Group, and how Maria asked him how he knows Hannah was dead, Perez is pacing the room, on his cell with I guess the cops who are out searching for Hannah with a hundred people going in the total wrong direction.

I tell Perez every detail I can remember Chuck mentioning in Group. I tell him about Hannah's seizures a few weeks before. He nods. "They put nasty shit in this street blow. Boric acid. Ketamine. Some people don't take too well to it."

At the end of the interview, Perez looks me in the eye. "You did good, kid. You did real good." I hang my head. I know I'm not a hero. I should have done much more, much sooner. But I know part of the reason I didn't help Hannah was I was afraid of her. I was afraid she would hate me for trying to stop her.

When Perez leaves, Barbara gives me a light hug. "So far, so good," she says. "Perez is one of the good guys. Good instincts. And you, my dear, are a good witness. You stay on point, focused." I nod, still not feeling worthy of praise.

"Are they going to arrest Chuck?" I ask. She nods.

"I believe they will. They'll need to determine cause of death first, assuming she is dead, which as you point out, we don't know. But Chuck is not in a good position. He's likely looking at manslaughter. Or felony endangerment."

I see why something should happen to Chuck. He let her die, or thought he did. He admits he hit a dying girl. But I want someone to know about Senna, too.

"None of this would have happened without Senna," I say. "In a way, Chuck was just unlucky. He was obsessed with Hannah."

Barbara looks at me and tilts her head. "Obsession is almost always narcissistic. The person can't accept rejection. They have too fragile a sense of self. It is not a genuine caring for another, but I agree that Chuck is a scapegoat here for some pretty nefarious characters. But I think Perez is your guy. No one likes a boyfriend who pimps out a girlfriend, or dealers branching out into sex work, or grown men assaulting teenaged girls."

I nod. It's true that I've done what I can. I've given them all I have.

However bad things have turned out for Chuck and Hannah, however they might unfold for Senna, I know there were times, lots of them, when they all looked down on me and Andy, and thought we were the losers, the followers, the leftover people. I definitely envied all of them—Hannah and Chuck for their beauty, Senna for his strange power over everyone. I idolized Hannah, it's true. But although I didn't do what I should have to help her, and although I may have even wanted to see them all crash, I never foresaw anything this terrible happening to any of them.

THIRTY-FOUR

IT'S BEEN WEEKS since Hannah was found. Senna and Chuck are both being charged by the police with felony reckless endangerment. I've heard from Barbara that Senna has agreed to give evidence against Alex in exchange for parole and community service, as well as, of course, treatment. Senna is back at school. He keeps to himself. He passes me in the hall as though I don't exist.

Chuck is going away to a treatment school upstate. He still has to go to court, but for now the judge has accepted a therapeutic educational facility that is locked down at night. He leaves in a few weeks. He is like a ghost. I see him when I go to the Center for counseling with a new therapist there named Angie. I don't go to the Group anymore. Kevin and Group are now just one part of the Center. They've hired two more traditional therapists and have another meeting with grown-ups as mediators, which is the one I attend. The police put pressure on the administration at the Center to provide more options for the kids who are sent there by the department. The police chief was not so pleased to hear about kids confessing in peer groups and advising other kids to conceal felony acts. Kevin called a meeting for all staff and kids, and explained the principle of peer counseling. "Kids understand kids. Especially these days, it's important that committed kids, kids who are truly sober, hear from other kids. The world is just changing too fast, and we can't always know all that's out there. That said, kids don't understand the law, or really the consequences of their actions, so all groups will have supervisors present once a week, and all kids can choose to attend only supervised groups." Kevin looked directly at me during certain parts of his speech. I've become one of the important kids.

At school, there has been a lot of talk about Chuck, how he tried to kill Hannah and then ran to the Center to make it seem like an under-the-influence accident. I believe his story, but not everyone does. What no one really considers is that she almost killed him, too. The papers call her an overdose victim, as though the coke came to her and hunted her down. They call her the victim of neglect, of criminal endangerment. There's been a lot in the news about drug rings in the suburbs, and how kids aren't as safe as they seem. There aren't a lot of details, though, about Senna and Chuck, since they're juveniles. But the webcam site and Alex and his partners have all been written about, like the lowlifes they are. The local paper says Hannah was lured by Alex, by "the promise of drugs." I don't know about that, exactly. Hannah might have been lured, but it was something in her, too, something smoldering, that maybe needed to burn itself out.

Andy and I walk into the hospital room together. The room is filled with flowers. There are no shades on the window and it is very bright. Outside, there's a construction site across from a busy intersection. Even with the window closed, we can hear the jackhammers. We're in the wing of the hospital for people with brain injuries. It is very quiet inside and very noisy outside. I think how silent our minds actually are, even when our thoughts are disturbing, or actually terrifying.

There's a single bed in the room, a high hospital bed with very white sheets. My immediate thought is we have the wrong room, and I can tell Andy thinks this too. In the high, narrow metal bed is a very still child. The child is neither male nor female in appearance. The child's face is very white. There are plastic tubes coming out of its nose. Its arms are connected by tubes to the metal IV stand next to the bed. The child's head is wrapped in white bandages. I gasp, because the child is so pale and beautiful.

Of course, this is Hannah.

The nose is long and straight. The mouth is hers—full lips, with a long upper lip that presses against the hollow cheeks and is punctuated by deep, somewhat uneven dimples. It is the resting mouth that should awaken into her crooked, too-wide, manic grin. But it doesn't move.

The eyes are somewhat sunken, but even closed you can see the shape is slightly square and large for the narrow face. These are Hannah's features, but stone-like and luminous. There is a beauty in her stillness that is not hers, not a part of Hannah's captivating grace. It is the simple beauty of something living at rest. The beauty of pumped blood and cell reproduction. I half expect the eyes to flash open and for the real Hannah to fill the room with her vibrancy. But this is the real Hannah.

I reach for Andy's hand.

We walk to her bedside together and sit in the two mauve-colored chairs. Her eyelids flutter. You can see the purplish veins just beneath the skin. There is a humming sound that comes from some unseen machine.

Hannah is no longer in a coma. Today is the first day we've been allowed to see her. All she does is sleep. We've been warned she may not recognize us. We've been told not to try too hard to get her to understand who we are and why we're there. She is confused. Her confusion makes her emotional. She's been given drugs to keep her calm, to help her cope with her memory loss. She, we are told, knows her mother, her own name, her address, and that she loves to sing. She has asked for her mom to play her favorite album by Bella Johnson, *My Life Cycles*. It's the music we used to listen to in her room, when we were alone, without the guys. Sometimes, we'd get stoned and she'd sing to it. There's a line I remember from a song called "Birth." *I can't always remember who you want me to be. I just keep guessing, and guessing taught me to believe.*

I don't know what Hannah will remember about our friendship or about Senna or Chuck, or about her thirst for more and more of whatever it was that got her off. I do hope she remembers every lonely hour until she was found by the shed off the trail in the woods up by the reservoir. I hope she remembers every hour of her near-death, when everyone in town was petrified. I remember the hours, the minutes, and the seconds. I remember not being able to wash time away with beer and vodka, and how still it stood, and how hard it was to push through. I can't help but feel in a strange way like Hannah is getting a sort of storybook ending. Who else gets to die and come back to life with all her crimes erased? Everyone loves second chances. I got mine, but through hard work and humiliation. Hannah has the drama of being the miracle girl. The miraculousness of her being alive seems to make everyone forget the crucial fact that Hannah was not anyone else's pure victim. She almost died, like I almost died, from something that at one time felt like a party.

Maybe Hannah's life will always be dramatic. Maybe she will become the star she wants to be—the great pop star, the next Bella Johnson. I don't doubt it. But I know, even if no one else does, the great case of the Missing Girl, the Mysterious Disappearance of Hannah Scott, is a sham. Like me, Hannah threw her life away with two hands. Hers swung like a boomerang back at her. It's not because she deserves it. She doesn't. But I don't think any of us deserves to be here in the first place, not until we do something decent with our lives, even if that one decent thing is accepting who we are. I don't need to be the most beautiful girl in school, or to have a guy like Chuck worship me. I'm okay now that it's just me and Andy.

Now here Hannah is—quiet, pale, like a sleeping baby, her skin almost pearl-like. It's as though she is about to emerge from some strange, mammalian chrysalis. But I know I shouldn't glamorize. This isn't really rebirth, not a real miracle—it's survival. Everybody does it.

Andy holds my hand, and after we sit by her bed for half an hour we lose hope that she'll wake up this time, and decide to leave.

Outside, the wind is fierce. We have to catch the subway downtown, head across town, and catch the Metro-North train back home. There's a little Spanish restaurant on the corner with pastries in the window and one of those neon-lit coffee cups with a cloud of electric white steam coming out of it. I nudge Andy when I see it, and we go in.

It's almost empty, and we sit at the counter on light blue vinyl stools. Andy picks up an old laminated menu, and the guy speaks to him in Spanish. This happens a lot to Andy even though he's Indian, Chinese, white, and zero Hispanic. But he takes Spanish in school and orders us both cafe con leche and points to the cheese Danishes on the shelf behind the counter.

The coffee is hot and the milk is slightly sour, like it's been on the stove a few hours. The Danish isn't fresh either. It's the kind they mass-produce in some plant somewhere, with heavy dough and a too-sweet, crumbly filling. But it's the first thing I've eaten in about five hours and I have to restrain myself to keep from devouring it in a few bites.

"It's actually not bad," I say between mouthfuls, and Andy nods.

"How you feeling?" I ask him.

"You mean about her?" he asks.

"Yeah," I say. "About Hannah."

"I think she's pretty lucky," he says. "Or pretty fucking unlucky, depending on how you look at it." I laugh.

"You could say that about any of us," I say. Andy looks at me. His eyes are so dark I sometimes can't see their expression, just my own reflection. I'm not sure he agrees with me. His brother, Jonas, is the only one of our group who's actually being prosecuted. He could go to jail for five years depending on the deal the prosecutor offers, and how much Jonas knows and is willing to spill about where all the coke was coming from, and who Alex's connections are. Andy's dad moved out for a while, but came back after a couple weeks on his own. Andy says his dad blames his mom for not raising them right. He says they still fight about how it was his mom who let Jonas go to his first high school party.

"I wonder who she's going to be when she wakes up," I say. "I mean when she really recovers."

Andy shrugs. "No idea. She'll have an army of people around her, I guess. Mega-support."

"I guess that'll be good for her," I say. My new therapist, Angie, tells me not to worry too much about Hannah, even though it's natural to feel bad, even guilty about where she is and what happened to her. But that wasn't what I felt sitting by her bed. Watching Hannah sleep, looking so small and frail, I wanted her to know where she was and who we were. I wanted her to know how long we've been waiting for her. Angie says it's normal to resent someone who is sick. I guess I can't tell how I'll really feel about Hannah until she starts talking again. Hannah has always seemed like an actress to me, acting in her own life, in her own daily drama. Her life never seemed as real as mine or as hard, because I worshipped her, put her above myself and everyone else I knew. I don't anymore. I guess I want her to wake up and know that I've moved on.

"Do you think she'll come back to Waverly?" Andy asks. "Or do you think she'll go somewhere like Chuck?"

"I don't know," I say. "I don't know what's better—having a second chance where everyone knows your story, or getting to start all over." Andy is quiet for a minute.

"Same story either way," he says.

Andy and I take the train back home and I fall asleep for most of the ride. My head is on his shoulder and I can feel a little drool in the corner of my mouth when I wake up, but he doesn't seem to notice.

Our bikes are locked up at the train station and I ask Andy to ride with me over to feed Michiko's cat. The bird died a week ago. Michiko says he was almost twenty years old. She buried him in the backyard in a shoebox. I was there and helped her dig the hole. She seemed pretty upset about it, actually. She even put on lipstick and a wide-brimmed black hat for the burial. Marco weaved between her legs as she lowered the box into the ground.

I was the one who found him dead in his cage. I called Michiko to tell her, and I could tell she was crying a little as she asked me to put him in a ziplock bag in the freezer. I was terrified to touch him, so I asked Andy to come over and help me out. Andy brought two pairs of knit gloves so we could lift him out of the cage together and slip him into the bag. "Remind me not to get old and weird," I said to Andy after I put the bird on the freezer shelf next to a package of organic chicken.

"It might be better than getting old and not-weird," Andy said. "Anyway, you probably don't have that much choice. You're pretty weird now, so . . ." I hit him with my glove, but then the hitting turned into kissing.

We ride through town and up over the hill near Senna's. We have a choice then—take the Death Wish down or go the long way around in the blustery wind.

When we reach the opening down to the path, we say nothing, just look. It's late afternoon and the sun will set in less than an hour. Even with the daylight and being sober, it's a challenging ride. I have a new bike, though, a real mountain bike my parents bought me for getting around town. They realized that since they've only just let me start to practice driving again, I'm not getting my license anytime soon, and my road bike is too fragile for the pot-holed side streets in our town.

Down the path, you can see the rocks, roots, and worst of

all, the wet leaves that make the path a slick obstacle course. It's funny how it's actually scarier when you can see everything in front of you. It's not a question, though. We both know we're going down it. With the wind kicking up and the clouds rolling in, it could be the last day before the path is covered in ice and snow. I inch up to the edge of the first steep drop. Somehow, both Andy and I know it's my day to lead.

AUTHOR'S NOTE

A GREAT DEAL of scientific research has been done in the last several years that is having an impact on how disordered drinking is addressed in both young people and adults. Scientists do not use the words "alcoholism" or "alcoholic," but instead use the term "alcohol use disorder." It is recognized that this is a spectrum disorder, and that not all people who misuse alcohol must abstain from alcohol permanently. Most people have heard about abstinence-only programs, which is the kind of program depicted in *The First True Thing*. However, there are many options that, unfortunately, most parents and young people are unaware of.

Below is a list of podcasts, articles, books, and websites I recommend for readers who are interested in learning about a range of options for the treatment of drug and alcohol dependency:

"Blame It on the Alcohol," On the Media, National Public
    Radio, February 9, 2018

"The Fix," Radiolab, National Public Radio, December 18,
    2015

"A Different Path to Fighting Addiction" by Gabrielle Glaser,
    New York Times, July 3, 2014

*Beyond Addiction: How Science and Kindness Help People
    Change* by Jeffrey Foote, Carrie Wilkens, Nicole Kosanke,
    and Stephanie Higgs, Scribner, 2014

*Inside Rehab: The Surprising Truth About Addiction
    Treatment—and How to Get Help That Works* by Anne M.
    Fletcher, Viking Penguin, 2013

The Center for Motivation and Change,
    www.motivationandchange.com

ACKNOWLEDGMENTS

I WOULD LIKE to express my thanks to my agent, Alice Tasman, and to my editors, Rosemary Brosnan and Jessica MacLeish, for their support, excellent suggestions throughout the writing process, and their keen attention to detail. I am also grateful to Bill Arkin for his expert and timely input, and to my daughters, as always, for their enthusiasm for a story (no matter how dark) and their always fearless feedback.